Disaster struck Robina when she lost her
lovely home and her beloved uncle in one
terrible night. There was little left now
of her old life—except for her abiding
detestation of Leo Morgan who was responsible for so much of her unhappiness.
And yet her new life seemed to be inex-
tricably involved with him . . .

CHAPTER ONE

THE night of the storm was one that Robina Jefferson would remember as long as she lived. It changed her life and it was the most terrible night she had ever known.

The weather had been sultry all week, due to break, due for a storm. The television had flashed that evening until Uncle Randolph advised her to turn it off, and then the radio had crackled, and she had curled into one of the big soft leather armchairs, reading a book, sipping a hot milky drink and nibbling biscuits and cheese.

Nothing had warned her what the night would bring. This was the room in which her days usually ended. For the last year it had usually been just herself and Uncle Randolph, and that was how it was that night. When the clock chimed half ten he got up, from his winged-back chair, and said, 'Well, I'm for bed.'

'Me too.' She was bored with her book, a library murder mystery. She was half way through and she still didn't care who the killer was.

'Fare thee well,' said Uncle Randolph. He always said that, every night, always had. He looked tired, but lately he had looked tired most of the time, and she smiled up at him, just as she did every night, and said, 'Goodnight.'

She should have said, 'Goodbye,' and told him how much she loved him, because it was her last chance. She should have taken his arm and got him out of the Castle. They should both have run for their lives, but she didn't know that then.

So she did what she always did—turned out the lights, and went to the window to pull back the long heavy

5

brocaded drapes, glanced across the bay at the house whose windows were still alight. In the Castle most of the rooms were closed and shuttered and never used, but everything in that house was thriving.

She walked in darkness to the kitchens, she knew every step of the way so well that she could have walked blindfolded, and left the supper tray—for morning, she thought. Then she climbed the wide oak staircase up to the gallery, and reached her bedroom.

It was a beautiful room, with watered silk wallpaper in the palest of pinks and even some Louis Quinze furniture. Several of the best pieces left to the family were in here, and Robina always felt relaxed when she came into her bedroom and closed the door behind her.

Lately there had been times when life had been grim. The Jeffersons were local aristocracy, but in the last few years their fortunes had gone downhill rapidly, and now it was a faded and threadbare façade they presented to the world.

Money still came in, from trusts, and Uncle Randolph would never discuss the question of selling and getting out. Anyhow, who would want a rambling pseudo-Gothic pile like this? It had been built by an early Victorian Jefferson on the site of their smaller Georgian home and was unconvertible for any practical purpose. So they shut rooms, lived in a kitchen and a small drawing room, and rattled around like dried peas in a large tin can.

Some day it would have to go, but Robina couldn't imagine living anywhere else. She had been born here, lived here all her life. She could remember the rooms filled with servants and friends. She knew the pictures that had covered those darker shapes on the wallpaper, the furniture that had gone, but she wasted no time on regret. She was young and strong and these were tough times for most folk, and when Christopher, her brother, said, 'You can't spend the rest of your life in this mausoleum, why doesn't the old man put it on the market? Somebody might want it,' she laughed.

'Nobody's made us an offer yet. I suppose we'll have to leave some day, but they'll carry me out of here screaming.'

Uncle Randolph had no thought of selling Cliffe Castle, and he certainly would never have taken Christopher's advice. He still blamed Chris for resigning from the family firm and following his star into the world of TV filming, although Chris had always hated clocking into an office, and the engineering business had bored him out of his mind.

Chris couldn't have saved the firm. The takeover would still have come if Chris had been seated on Uncle Randolph's right hand at the conference table, instead of being the other side of the world, filming in Abu Dhabi. But the gulf between the two she loved best grieved Robina. Chris took it cheerfully enough, but his 'desertion' still rankled with Uncle Randolph, who was always very much on his dignity when Christopher came home.

Not that the Castle was Chris's home any more. Only Robina and Randolph Jefferson lived here now. The domestic quarters were empty. Until last month there had been a woman who helped with the housework and a man who helped in the garden, but they had moved on after a six-month stay, and Robina couldn't blame them.

The wages were fair, but there was so much needing to be done that it was overwhelming. Except for a vegetable patch the gardens were almost entirely grass and trees now, ending in a zig-zag path down the cliffs to the beach, but gardeners grew bored with eternally mowing lawns; and with all those closed doors and shuttered rooms working inside the Castle could be depressing.

It wasn't so long ago that things had been so different. When Robina and Christopher came home from their boarding schools the Castle had been a return to Camelot.

The holidays had been glorious adventures with the great house to run riot in, the sea and the rugged Cornish coastline for their playground, and Uncle Randolph, courtly and wise and kind, like Merlin and King Arthur in one man.

She had had a wonderful childhood. Boarding school wasn't bad, but she couldn't wait to leave and come home and take over the running of the Castle. She could have done it well. She could have arranged the dinner parties and the business lunches, organised the kitchens and the kitchen gardens, made the house even more beautiful, the grounds even lovelier. But it seemed that no sooner was she home for good than the axe fell.

It must have been hovering, swinging around up there. But when Robina and Christopher were at school they had never noticed. Chris was twelve months older than Robina. They had been orphaned as babies and reared by their uncle, and it had always been accepted that Christopher would go into the family engineering firm and Robina would run the house.

Nobody asked Chris if that was what he wanted to do, although his passion was photography from when he got his first camera and set up a dark room in one of the storerooms right at the top of the castle.

Robina was twenty-two now. Eighteen months ago Chris had walked out. Six months later the works had been taken over, but he couldn't have prevented that. It was a good thing he was making a success doing work he enjoyed, because the golden days were over for the Jeffersons of Cliffe Castle.

Robina ran the Castle all right—nearly single-handed. The cooking, and the cleaning, and the gardening. If there had been a lodge they would probably have been living in that. She was very busy, and fairly happy. She took each day as it came, although since the takeover, that had left

Uncle Randolph with a nominal seat on the board and no real power or real work to do, she had worried about him.

He was a shadow of what he used to be, and she didn't think about the future. She just fought her battle of keeping the grass down, and the rooms they used habitable, and shut her mind to what next month or next year might bring. Much as she shut the doors of all those other rooms. She knew that some were empty and the rest were shrouded with dust sheets, but if she never opened the doors it wasn't too hard to pretend that they were still like they used to be.

The storm started while she was undressing. She heard thunder rolling in from the sea and decided not to draw back the curtains. She didn't care much for storms. If she couldn't see the lightning she stood a better chance of getting to sleep. She was drowsy, and she yawned, stretching, slipping a pink cotton nightdress over her head.

The reflection in the oval old Italian mirror showed a girl who looked taller than she was. She had a lithe body, long legs, long neck. Ankle bones and hands were narrow. A well bred lady, recognisable in a dozen portraits and miniatures scattered around the house, going back over three hundred odd years. And a beauty. Her hair was a dark cloud, her face a pale oval. She had blue eyes, fringed by thick dark lashes, a straight nose and a mouth that closed firmly, a cleanly chiselled mouth over small white even teeth.

Her expression was usually calm and grave. She looked serene, hard to ruffle, but not one to trifle with because even in a multiple store cotton nightdress, barefoot and ready for bed, Robina Jefferson seemed a lady who appreciated her own worth and position and expected the rest of the world to do likewise.

But her smile could be a surprise. It could transform her; showing a touch of mischief, a touch of wildness, that made you wonder if the calm perfect face was a mask hiding the real girl.

She realised soon enough that there would be no sleeping through this storm. By the time it was overhead it sounded like hell let loose. Even with her hands over her ears she was almost deafened by the never-ending thunder, and she knew that lightning was shearing the sky and reflecting jagged white on the churning black sea.

She felt the strike, like nothing she had ever known, a terrifying hissing crackle. She started up wildly, and then hunched back on to her bed and stayed there for a minute or two trying to calm herself. She knew that lightning had hit them, but after the crash she anticipated no immediate danger.

The Castle was a very large house. This was unpleasant and scarey, because something nasty had happened somewhere. Goodness knows where, there were countless possibilities: tall turrets and mock battlements with ornate baroque railings, statuary, and rods that had once flown pennants on pinnacles reaching to the sky. Probably the damage wouldn't be visible till morning. She expected it to be confined to one small isolated spot.

But she couldn't stay up here any longer. There was no chance of sleep until the storm passed. She was going downstairs and she hoped that Uncle Randolph would be joining her because she was feeling jittery.

The din was indescribable, the crashing thunder and a great roaring that must be the wind. Robina daren't touch the electric switch, so she went across to the windows, to open the curtains and let in enough light to pick up a dressing gown and slippers. But before she could reach the window her bedroom door was flung open. Smoke poured in as her uncle staggered gasping, 'Robina, quickly!'

The roaring was fire. She could smell it, feel it. The gallery behind him was rosy grey. 'Oh God!' she sobbed and together they plunged through the choking fumes, stumbling, almost falling down the wide staircase. Reaching the bottom, they stared at each other, caught in the same nightmare. Flames roared above them and Robina said jerkily, 'I must phone the fire brigade.'

'No time.' Her uncle gripped her arm and dragged her along, and he was right. The smoke was following like a creeping poisonous fog. The house was a death-trap, and they flung themselves on the great door, hurling back bolts, turning the key, lurching out into the night.

Robina stopped after a few steps to look up, and again her uncle grabbed her arm, urging her on until they were well away from the debris that was falling, trailing clouds of sparks.

They stopped not far from the pathway down the cliffs, then they turned and looked, and the middle of the Castle was burning, from the open door through which they had just escaped to the height of the little stone towers, up there edging the main roof. Every window was bright alight and Robina thought crazily, The last time I saw a light in every window I must have been about sixteen. Christmas, I think it was. She said, 'Why doesn't the rain put out the flames?'

Her uncle said nothing and she touched her face and it was hardly raining at all. These were tears pouring down her cheeks, from the smoke in her eyes and from watching the Castle die. She had never known such anguish nor such helplessness. They stood very close together, staring as though it was a spectacle, a firework display, and neither said a word.

Someone would come before long. A beacon like this would be seen for miles. Everybody would know it was the Castle, somebody would phone for help, but it would be too late, it was too late already.

Robina could never have said how long they stood there

before she heard the sirens. Probably only about fifteen minutes, but if she had been told it was hours she would have agreed. After the first fire engine and police car there seemed to be crowds of people, all of them running, shouting. Cars and people everywhere.

And the rain came deluging down, although she hardly noticed it. It was more like hell than ever, the rain and the flames and the dark darting figures. Some faces were friends who walked up and down with her and said how terrible it was. Somebody put a coat round her shoulders and somebody else put shoes on her feet, and ladders were shooting up and hoses were playing, but the flames still went on roaring and leaping. The ladders and the men looked like toys against an inferno. It was no contest, there was never any chance that the little puppet figures might win.

She thought this had to be the worst thing that could happen to her, until there was more shouting, more running, and someone came dashing up and said, 'It's your uncle. He's collapsed.'

She had been dazed, but that brought her into sharp awareness, and she ran over to the firefighting equipment, between the vehicles drawn up on the lawns, to where Randolph Jefferson lay.

They held her back gently when she reached him. There was an oxygen mask over his face. In the weird flickering of the fire and the blue flashing lights of the police car they were fighting for his life, and they went on fighting. But again it was a battle that no man could win. He had had a slight coronary a few months earlier. This time it was massive and murderous. He had died as he gasped and fell . . .

Robina woke in a strange room. She must have seen it last night when they brought her here, but it was strange to her this morning. Her head was aching and she remembered everything that had happened and her breath caught as she struggled to sit up. She had taken sleeping pills. First she had tried to phone Christopher, but he hadn't been there, and the girl called Sarah Morgan had taken the telephone from Robina's hand and given a number and said it was vital that he should ring here as soon as possible.

'Here' was Sarah Morgan's home, the house across the bay. Robina had known that Uncle Randolph was dead, when the men bending over him straightened and looked at her, and after that it hadn't mattered to her where she went. She had to tell Christopher, and Sarah was close by and Robina had let herself be driven away in Sarah's car, and that was how she had come to this house.

When there was no Christopher at the other end of the line there was Dr Buxton, who had been their family doctor for years, standing beside her. 'Take this,' he had said, and she had taken the glass and the little white tablets, and swallowed greedily because the only thing she craved at that moment was oblivion.

She never wanted to wake up, but she was waking now and Sarah Morgan was coming across the room towards the bed. She wanted to close her eyes again and sink back and feign sleep. She couldn't bear the pity that was going to be offered. She shouldn't have let them bring her here. She should have kept away from people, hidden somewhere until the pain was less. She must hold back the pain until she was alone. She mustn't break down before strangers.

Sarah Morgan looked as though she hadn't slept. There were shadows under her red-rimmed eyes and her soft fair hair fell over her face, tangled as though she hadn't washed it since she was out in the rain last night. She was a pretty girl. Uncle Randolph always said she reminded him of a china doll. You didn't see many china dolls these days, but Robina knew what he meant.

When Sarah reached the bedside her eyes were brimming with tears, and one slid down her smooth round cheek. Robina's own eyes were dry, and she thought, I'm feeling nothing. I mustn't feel or I shall start screaming and never stop.

'Are you all right?' Sarah whispered, as though they mustn't be overheard, and Robina nodded and thought, What a stupid question!

'I'll get you some coffee.' Sarah's voice was still hardly more than a croak.

'Thank you,' said Robina.

'Your brother phoned, but we thought it best not to wake you. He should be here quite soon.'

'Thank you,' said Robina again. It was morning now. Daylight poured in through the windows. The room was beautiful—modern and all of a piece, as though it had been designed by a top name and everything bought to fit into the decor. You saw rooms like this in magazines and wondered whether anyone actually lived in them.

She remembered her own bedroom, and it seemed a long way away, dreamlike. Everything seemed dreamlike, this room too. The soft bed with the silken sheets, the girl moving soundlessly over the thick carpet.

There was a light knock on the door and a tray was handed in and Sarah carried it to a small table beside the bed. Now how did she tell them we were ready for coffee? Robina wondered muzzily. Telepathy? Or did she press a bell somewhere? 'Please,' she said when Sarah asked, 'Cream? Sugar?' although she usually took her coffee without either.

Her hands were steady, but cold. She sipped the coffee and Sarah stood looking at her, biting a lip, worried and indecisive. 'Dr Buxton said I was to call him when you woke,' Sarah said at last.

'What time is it?' asked Robina.

'Just after half past seven.'

'Don't bother him yet. I expect he has a surgery and he must have had a very late night.' Robina listened to her own voice, light and cool, and it was as though someone else was speaking. Someone sensible enough so that was all right, she didn't want doctors fussing around as though she was an invalid.

'I'd like to get up,' she said, 'but I suppose I have no clothes.'

'I put these out for you.' There was a long sofa where Sarah was pointing and when Robina blinked and concentrated she saw a grey skirt, a harebell cashmere sweater and a small pile of undies. 'I think you're taller than I am,' Sarah was apologising about that, 'but perhaps they'll do for now.'

'Thank you,' said Robina, as Sarah opened a door showing a bathroom. Having done that Sarah bit on her lip again and hesitated, and Robina assured her, 'I'm safe to be left.'

'Yes, of course you are,' Sarah agreed hastily. 'I'll be in the next room. When you're ready, or if you want anything, just tap on the wall.'

'Thank you.' Those two words were becoming an automatic response, although Robina had never had less to be thankful for in her life. She watched Sarah leave the room, and then she put the half empty cup on the tray and pushed back the sheet and duvet. It took an effort, although the duvet was the lightest of down.

When she stood she swayed, then she steadied herself and walked slowly towards the open door of the bathroom. She was wearing someone else's nightdress. Hers had been cotton, this was crêpe-de-chine. Someone must have changed her and washed her last night, or perhaps she had done it herself. She couldn't remember too clearly, and she didn't want to remember.

The bathroom was an extension of the bedroom, the

same colour scheme, the same tiny blue daisies on the wallpaper. Nothing personal about it, no clutter in the cabinets. Fresh towels, fresh soap, fresh tissues. It could be an hotel bathroom, five star, of course. Perhaps she could pretend it was an hotel, and she looked at her reflection, the mask-face paper pale.

She daren't get into the bath—she might slip under, although perhaps that wouldn't be too bad a thing—and she turned the shower to lukewarm, blood heat, because she didn't want to shock herself awake. This haze was better. She wanted it to last as long as possible. She closed her eyes as the water ran over her face and opened them reluctantly when she stepped out of the shower.

She towelled, then went back to the bedroom. The clothes fitted well enough. Sarah was slightly plumper but not much shorter. Robina crossed to the dressing table picked up an ivory and silver backed brush and began to brush her still-damp hair very slowly.

She sat on the stool, her back to the mirror, wondering how long it would be before Chris came. Had they told him everything? They must have done, and it would be a terrible journey for him. She hoped he would drive carefully. He wasn't a careful driver, but surely he would take no chances this time. Perhaps he would bring Laura with him and she would drive.

He would be surprised to find his sister in this house. She was surprised herself, more surprised than Chris would be because Chris didn't really know—— A tap on the door scattered her thoughts and before she could call, 'Come in,' Sarah was in the room. She had a towel tied round her head and a little make-up on her face, just a touch of colour.

'The phone's started ringing,' she said. 'I've told them to take numbers and say you're still resting. Everyone's very concerned about you.'

'How kind of them,' said Robina, without irony because it was kind. Useless but kind.

'I didn't think you'd want to talk?' That sounded like a question, and Robina said,

'I don't. Only to Chris.'

'Would you like to stay in here until he comes or shall we go down?'

'It doesn't matter.'

'Shall we go down, then?' A hint of pleading in Sarah's voice meant that she would prefer downstairs, perhaps with other people around, and Robina agreed,

'Of course.'

She wasn't seeing anything too clearly. She followed Sarah, getting an impression of space and light. She had never been in this house before and Uncle Randolph had described it as, 'All right if you like that kind of thing.' It was small, compared to the Castle, but less claustrophobic. There seemed to be more windows and fewer shadows.

The room into which Sarah took her was cool and elegant, with Chinese carpets, and chair covers and curtains in the same delicate pastel shades. Robina stood stock still just inside the room, even the decision of which chair to sit on seemed beyond her, and Sarah asked anxiously, 'Are you all right? Is there anyone you'd like me to call for you? Or fetch?'

There had to be people she would rather be with right now than this comparative stranger, but she couldn't call them to mind. 'Not at the moment, thank you,' she said, 'I'll just wait until my brother comes.'

Sarah was weeping again. She blinked and fat tears squeezed between her lashes, but Robina's tears were frozen deep inside her. She might break down when Christopher came, but she hoped not. Breaking down wouldn't bring the dead to life.

She shut her mind against the word 'dead', because she

couldn't believe that Uncle Randolph had gone. She
wouldn't believe it. She walked slowly and carefully to one
of the big windows, where the curtains hung in milky folds,
and looked out across the bay. The sea was calm as a mill-
pond and the skies were cloudless. There was a boat out
there and she wondered if it had been out during the
storm. If it had they would have a tale to tell, although in
an hour or two on a day like this last night's weather
would be forgotten. A bit of excitement and no harm done.

She had to force herself to look directly across, to the
highest spot on the skyline on which the Castle stood,
and when she did she gasped aloud. She had thought there
would be nothing left, but at first sight the silhouette
seemed unchanged, and then she remembered that stone
doesn't burn. It was probably just a shell, but from here the
Castle could be like those rooms behind the closed doors.
She could pretend that everything was all right in there.
Even that Uncle Randolph was sitting at the window in
the little drawing room, taking breakfast—coffee, toast,
occasionally bacon and eggs.

Sarah touched her arm almost timidly and asked, 'Would
you—could I get you something to eat?'

'What? No. No, thank you.'

She kept her eyes on the outline of her home and Sarah
said, 'You can hardly tell, can you?' realising at once how
abysmally tactless that had been, remembering that Randolph Jefferson had died. 'I——' she stammered, 'I
mean——'

'Not from here,' said Robina, and to Sarah's relief she
turned away from the window and sat down in a chair by
the fireplace. She was exhausted, although she must have
slept for hours. Her hands lay heavy in her lap and her
eyelids drooped and Sarah said,

'The doctor left some pills. He said if you needed them
they're just tranquillisers.'

Robina was tranquil enough. She still felt drugged. 'Probably later,' she said. 'I'll just sit here if I may, and wait.'

'You're sure there's nothing?' Sarah's sweet anxious face floated in front of her and she said firmly,

'Nothing at all.'

'You're very brave,' sighed Sarah, and Robina thought, What a fool the girl is; because this had nothing to do with courage. Some defence mechanism in her body was anaesthetising her mind, and for that she was grateful.

She was very cold, although it had to be a warm day and a warm room. She breathed shallowly, and it was too much of an effort to move. She could sit here like this for hours if she had to, waiting for Christopher to come.

He was all the family she had now, but they had always been close even after he went away. Almost every time they met he'd asked her to come and share his London flat. She had been up there on holiday and had fun. His friends would have accepted her, they seemed to like her. Laura, Chris's live-in girl-friend, had said there was plenty of room, and there was. Chris had a bargain, the top floor of an Edwardian house at the foot of Richmond Hill. But Robina had never wanted to stay. She had enjoyed holidaying there, but she had always been happy to come home.

Now there was no home, but she couldn't think about the future, and she sat still as a statue, stunned almost mindless by shock, until she heard the sound of a car.

It might not be Christopher, but it might be, and she watched the door and when Sarah opened it she looked at the man with her. She was too numb even for disappointment that it should be this man, not Chris. This was his house, one should expect to find him here.

Leo Morgan, Sarah's half-brother, seemed to fill the doorway. Big, broad-shouldered, with a thatch of jet black

hair, hooked nose, dark eyes. Any blood relationship between him and blonde china-doll Sarah seemed incredible,
but that was how it was.

Robina had moved slightly forward in her chair, now she
slumped back, and Leo Morgan looked at her, from glittering eyes under thick brows, analytic as a doctor. She wondered what he would say—how terrible it all was, or would
he ask again if she was all right?

He said, 'There's nothing I can say,' and that was true,
'except please stay here. Use this house as long as you
need it.'

'Thank you.' Her lips were as dry as her eyes. 'That's
very neighbourly of you.'

He looked *rich*. His clothes were always discreet. He
was in a white silk shirt and a perfectly cut dark suit, but
you knew—just looking at him—that everything he wore
was the best. Uncle Randolph called him 'the pirate' and
Robina could easily imagine him in the flamboyant clothes
of Captain Morgan: the velvets and laces, the plumed hat,
the great boots and swaggering cape. She felt a faint
tremor of dislike and turned her head, then she heard him
go out of the room and Sarah came over to her chair asking again, 'Anything you want?'

'No, thank you.' Nothing that you can get for me.

Other cars came. She heard them. And then at last one
of them was Christopher's and he came rushing into the
room shutting the door behind him on Sarah who was following, as Robina jumped up and stumbled into his arms.

They looked alike, this brother and sister. Christopher's
hair was shorter and curly, but they had the same features,
the same blue eyes. A head taller than Robina, Christopher
was a strikingly handsome young man, although now his
face was old with grief. They clung together as though
they could draw support from each other. 'Bina-baby,' he
whispered. 'Don't cry, love, don't cry.'

Bina had been her pet name as a baby. No one had used it for years, and she wasn't crying, she couldn't cry. Chris had always been more extrovert than Robina, less reserved. She didn't want to talk about Uncle Randolph at all, but he said, 'Poor old chap, at least it was quick.'

'It shouldn't have happened.' She spoke through clenched teeth and he sighed and held her tighter. 'No, but thank God you're all right.'

'I wouldn't have been if he hadn't come for me.' Some time she might blame herself for not having discovered the fire sooner. The rush along to her room, the frantic flight to safety, must all have added to the strain on his heart. 'I owe him my life,' she said. 'I didn't know we were on fire.'

'We both owe him,' said Chris. 'I'm sorry I didn't always see things his way.'

'He loved you, though. He loved both of us.' They must always remember that, because it was all they had left. Robina looked across at the window, and he followed her eyes and her thoughts and asked,

'What's the damage over there?'

'I don't know. I should think it's pretty well burned out.' She closed her eyes as though someone had led her to the window. 'I don't want to look. Not yet.'

'Sure,' said Chris. When she was a child she had fallen cliff climbing and needed six stitches in her leg. 'Don't look,' Chris had said, and he had held her tight, the way he was holding her now. 'You don't need to look,' he said now. 'I'll see to everything.'

There was a great deal to be done, but Chris shielded Robina from most of it. They both stayed in Leo Morgan's house. There were several guest rooms and Sarah had had one prepared for Christopher, and Robina got through the next few days with the details of the night of the storm almost completely blocked out of her mind.

She never answered the telephone. When Chris was

around and it was a call for the Jeffersons he took it.
Otherwise Sarah took messages, and when friends and
neighbours came to the house Robina sat, quiet and com-
posed, accepting condolences but feeling no real involvement.

She went shopping with Sarah, buying a strictly limited
wardrobe, something plain for the funeral, but even the
funeral didn't seem real. She and Chris stood hand in hand
and she could never have said who else was there nor given
a clear account of the ceremony.

Afterwards the will was read, by a solicitor in a panelled
office overlooking the square, and Robina watched sea-
gulls flying and sometimes settling on rooftops and wondered why they were bothering with this farce of legal
tradition. She was the sole heiress. Everything her uncle
had owned was for her. But the trust payments had ended
with his death, and the Castle had burned, so what did it
matter whose name was on that piece of paper?

But she listened, and shook hands with several people
afterwards, and when they went on about the kind of man
Uncle Randolph was, what a loss to the community, she
said, 'Yes indeed.' Then Chris took her downstairs and
round to the car park and opened the car door, and when
they were both sitting he said, 'Well, it's all over now, love.'

He meant the first few days, the inquest and the
funeral, not the grieving, although he hoped that it was
getting more bearable for her. It was for him. He was still
mourning Uncle Randolph, but he had to drive back to
London tonight; work wouldn't wait any longer. He asked,
'What are you going to do about the Castle?'

'I don't know.'

She hadn't been near. Chris had. Everybody she knew
seemed to have gone looking. She had heard a dozen times
that the fire had gutted the main part of the building so

that no one could live there again. Perhaps it could sell at site value.

Chris put a hand over hers. 'I'm glad what there is is left to you,' he said. 'Of course there'll be death duties to raise, but you ought to get something out of it.'

Robina shrugged slightly and he sighed. Her continued calm was worrying him. He would have felt easier if she had cracked up, it would have seemed more natural. She was a tough kid, always had been, perhaps she was doing her crying alone, but the time had come when she had to make up her mind about her future. 'I'll arrange to get the stuff valued,' he said. What had been salvaged was being stored in the outhouses.

'Would you do that?' she asked.

'Sure, that's easy enough. I've got to go back today, you know.' She nodded. 'Now, are you coming with me?'

He was offering her a home and surely she could find a job of some sort in London. But the prospect of the noise and bustle of the city, and Chris's friends and colleagues, with their jokes and their in-talk and their sharp minds, made her cringe. Later perhaps when she was strong again. She said, 'I don't want to leave here yet.'

She had been invited to stay in several houses, there had been offers of help from friends all around. Chris knew there had so perhaps he wouldn't argue. He didn't, he said, 'I expected that. Sarah was asking me yesterday about your plans. I think she'd like to discuss them with you.'

'Sarah Morgan? Why is she interested in my plans? Why was she talking about them to you? Why not to me?' and Chris said gently,

'Because you're not hearing too well these days, are you?'

'I suppose not,' she had to admit. She must drag herself out of this deep-frozen limbo, start feeling and living again.

She said, 'Very well, let's go and see Sarah.'

Sarah was at home. She had been at the funeral, but now she was standing in the doorway of the big white house, looking up the drive that curved from the road, and they all went into the light bright drawing room. Sarah was wearing a plain dark grey flannel suit and she looked like an eager schoolgirl, perching on the edge of a chair, 'Well?' she demanded of Christopher, who smiled,

'If you're interested in the will he left everything to Robina. If you want to know what Robina's plans are— she doesn't want to come to London.'

'I didn't think you would.' Sarah's head swivelled towards Robina. She sounded pleased, a little triumphant. 'I mean, your roots are in these parts aren't they, but you can't go back to the Castle, can you? And I know you've friends around who'd like to have you stay with them, but why don't you stay with me here?'

Robina smiled, puzzled. A permanent invitation was a pretty big thing, especially from a girl she had really only known by hearsay until a week ago. 'I'm supposed to be running this house,' Sarah went on. 'You could help me.'

'You want a housekeeper?' Robina could handle a job like that, but Sarah shook her head.

'No, we've got a housekeeper. I want a companion.' She leaned forward, hands clasped as though she was pleading. 'It would be a real job, with a salary, and it would give you a breathing space, wouldn't it?'

It was a tempting offer. Staying here for a while would give her the chance to get herself together, but there was one big obstacle, and she asked, 'What would your brother say about this? He's been very kind, putting us both up, but what would he think about you paying me to stay on?'

Sarah's smile was radiant. 'Oh, but I asked him, of course, and he thinks it's a fine idea. He thinks you'd be a good influence on me, you know, calm and sensible and cool.'

You don't know me very well, thought Robina, and neither does your brother. She looked across at her own brother and Chris was nodding encouragement. 'Are you sure about that?' said Robina.

'Honestly.' Now Sarah was extremely grave. 'I promise you, Leo approves. Salary and everything.'

'I'd have to have a word with him first.' She would want to hear from the man himself before she took up residence in his home.

'Right now,' said Sarah gleefully, and bounced off her chair, and Robina followed her down the hall to a door on which she tapped. The room was a study, a small library, a home office, and Leo Morgan sat behind a large desk with some foolscap typed pages spread out in front of him. As they went in Sarah said, 'I've been asking Robina to stay on and she wants to know how you feel about it.'

He smiled at them both, his teeth very white against the dark skin. 'All right,' he said to Sarah, 'run along,' and she did, without a word of protest.

He's treating her like a child, thought Robina. Why does she stand for it? She sat down, when he came round the desk and drew a chair forward for her, and then she said, 'I've just been offered a job here.'

'Yes?' He seemed to know all about it.

'Is there really a job or is Sarah being kind?'

He went back to his chair, which meant that he was facing her, and she had never seen such dark eyes, black as the pit, and yet Sarah's were wide and clear and limpid. He said, 'It's Sarah's suggestion, but I agree that she does need a companion.'

'Surely not?' Robina's lips twitched in the faintest of smiles. Everyone knew that Sarah Morgan was as popular as she was pretty. Uncle Randolph used to chuckle, 'What's our little china doll up to now?' when he saw her picture or her name on the gossip page.

Her latest escapade had been in Spain, where Leo Morgan had a villa and Sarah had met a handsome young fisherman. It must all have been idyllic until Leo descended on them and carted Sarah back here. That could only have happened a week or two ago, Robina and Uncle Randolph had smiled at that together.

'My sister isn't always circumspect in her choice of companions,' said Leo Morgan drily.

Her choice of men, he meant! At twenty-one Sarah could have passed for a virginal seventeen-year-old, but she had made a disastrous marriage on her eighteenth birthday against her brother's wishes. And I'll bet he never lets her forget it, thought Robina. She felt the glimmerings of pity for Sarah, who had been very sweet to her this week, very kind.

Leo Morgan was saying, 'I want her to stay down here for a while,'—no more globetrotting for Sarah. 'You'll be an ideal companion for her.'

'That's very flattering.'

Was it a companion he wanted for his sister or a jailor? she wondered. Or perhaps a spy? Someone to keep an eye on Sarah, that was for sure, so that he could break up any relationship that didn't have his approval. Sarah's young fisherman wouldn't have stood much chance when Captain Morgan sailed into town.

He went on talking about a salary—a good one—welcoming her to the household, offering any assistance she needed in the settling of her affairs; and he was a man with resources to cope with most problems.

It seemed to Robina that he exuded power, just sitting there. She looked him straight in the face and thought, you have a cruel mouth. You talk of help, but there's no compassion in you. You made Uncle Randolph old before his time. You caused that earlier heart attack. If he hadn't been weakened by that perhaps the last one wouldn't have killed him.

Feeling was coming back to her, the layers of ice were melting. But the first rush of emotion wasn't grief. It would be. She would weep for the man who had been a father to her, but what she felt now, in every nerve of her body, was a blinding hate.

CHAPTER TWO

ROBINA was taking the job as Sarah Morgan's companion, and everyone would say how lucky she was. The engineering firm that had belonged to her family since Victorian days was now part of the Leo Morgan empire, but nobody knew how Uncle Randolph had suffered because of that, nor how entrenched was Robina's resentment against this man who would be paying her monthly salary, and in whose home she would be living.

Uncle Randolph had put on a brave face over the take-over, but from the first rumours he had started to look haggard, in unguarded moments when he was alone with Robina. It happened so quickly. As fast as the speed with which the big white house had sprung up, where there had previously been a little chalet, used for summer lettings by an owner who made a tidy profit selling out to Leo Morgan.

When Robina saw the first bulldozers, moving like Martian monsters on the hillside across the bay, she had gasped, 'My God, he's not building himself a home here, is he?' and Uncle Randolph, standing beside her at a window of the Castle, had sighed, 'I'm afraid it looks very much like that, my dear. The pirate has come to stay.'

On the surface it was a civilised takeover arrangement. The shareholders voted for it enthusiastically. Leo Morgan was a tycoon who couldn't go wrong, of course they wanted him in charge of their affairs. But being thrown out, and he was thrown out although everybody pretended he was ready to stand down, crushed Uncle Randolph's spirit.

Only Robina knew that. She saw him come home, from meetings and conferences, looking grey and old. And the

28

first heart attack—that the doctors said had been caused by overwork, so it was lucky he had retired less than a month before because now he could take things easy—that was a broken heart.

One night he wept. Robina had gone out into the Castle garden looking for him, and walked silently over the turf to where she saw him under a clump of trees. He was very still, standing with folded arms, his tall straight figure bowed as though a weight was on his shoulders. The takeover was about to be finalised and she knew he was unhappy about it, but when she reached him she was horrified to see the glint of tears on his cheeks. She had never known him weep before. He was a proud, self-contained man. It was inexpressibly dreadful to her, and if she could have done she would have crept away. But he had seen her and she asked, 'Does it have to go through?'

·'It has gone through,' he said. 'From the moment Leo Morgan decided he wanted our little company there was no stopping him.'

She had heard all the reasons why they should become a small cog in Morgan's immense machine, and she said desperately, 'Then let him have it. He's not getting such a bargain.' Theirs was no longer a prosperous business and from all reports it was going downhill fast, but Uncle Randolph smiled faintly.

'You don't think he's getting a good deal? Oh, but he is. He has the Midas touch. Anything he buys turns to gold, so it has to be a bargain.'

He had had a meeting that day with Morgan, just the two of them, and Robina knew that in some way Uncle Randolph's pride had been cut from under him. She realised that this was the day when Leo Morgan had told him there was no place for him in the new set-up. She suspected as much then and she began to talk about the future, the things that Uncle Randolph would have time for now, a round of golf, travel, but he said quietly, 'The old firm was all I had to show for my life.'

She protested, '*No!* What about the army? What about the war?'

He had been a young captain at the storming of Cassino, but he shook his head slowly. 'That happened to another man a long time ago. No, the business was my life's work and no one can say I've made a success of that.'

Robina would have contradicted him, but it would have been such an obvious lie that it would have been no comfort. 'I know it's losing ground,' he said, as though he was talking to himself rather than to her. 'I've had that pointed out to me, and my part in the breakdown, but I would have liked to hand over to a gentleman.' He had looked at her then, with another smile that was no smile at all. 'Not to a pirate.'

She had felt as though she had been with him that afternoon, listening to Leo Morgan. She had known exactly what the interview must have been like, and she had looked across the bay, to where the new white house was rising and the earth was overturned where the gardens would be, and hoped passionately that Leo Morgan's luck would turn sour. She had wanted him hurt as badly as he was hurting the gentlest man she knew.

She had never forgiven him for the way he had treated Uncle Randolph, and she had seen him as rarely as possible. Several times, before the takeover, he had come to the Castle, but Robina had usually kept out of the way. It had always been business talk and she had never liked him. Afterwards she caught occasional glimpses of him in the gardens of his new home. He didn't seem to go down on the beach much. He had a boat, she supposed he was off on that when she saw it anchored out in deep water.

Sarah had only stayed here briefly until now, but she

had gone across to the Castle just after the white house was built, just after the takeover.

'I'm your new neighbour,' she had said, and Robina had been struck by her Marilyn Monroe prettiness, but unable to feel any warmth towards a girl who was Leo Morgan's sister. Robina had been polite, offering drinks, listening to Sarah's bubbling chatter and parrying invitations to the white house, but Sarah didn't come calling again.

She must have sensed the coolness, and anyway she was off within a few days. This wasn't the Morgans' only home. There was a London house, other houses in other countries, and Sarah led a jet-set life. From then on Robina and Uncle Randolph had followed her social career in the newspapers and from the gossip of the neighbours.

Robina would never have considered Sarah Morgan her friend, but Sarah had been among the first to dash across on the night of the storm, to see if she could help; and since then she couldn't have been more caring if they had been friends for a lifetime.

Robina was realising now that she had become very fond of Sarah. It would have been easy enough for Sarah to bring her back here and arrange for her to be looked after. There was staff in this house who presumably looked after guests. But Sarah had sat up all night by Robina's bed, and cried her eyes red. She had hardly let Robina out of her sight since, and she had been sensitive enough to know how it would help if Chris stayed here too, she had fixed that. Now she was inviting Robina to stay on as her companion. It wasn't only in looks that she differed from her brother. She was genuinely sympathetic. She wouldn't willingly hurt anyone, and if ever she needed an ally against Leo Morgan she had found one in Robina.

He was coming round the desk now. The interview was

over. He held out a hand, settling the deal, and Robina could hardly bear to touch him. His fingers could have crushed hers as her hand lay still in his. His grip was brief but even so it was an effort to repress a shudder.

'Welcome to the family,' he said. 'I'm sure Sarah's found a good friend in you.'

'I hope so,' said Robina, and thought how odd it was that he couldn't sense how she felt about him. Surely he had to be a judge of people to have made such a success of all his enterprises, but then of course he wasn't offering her a job where she could really foul up anything. If she had applied to work a machine he would have checked her qualifications. If she had been trying to get in on the executive side he would have made very sure that her interests coincided with his.

But a couple of minutes' conversation was all that was needed here. She looked and sounded like a lady, and she was Miss Jefferson of Cliffe Castle—what was left of it; and Sarah liked her and wanted her around. Leo Morgan didn't think she could do him any harm, nor did he see why she should bear him a grudge.

Nobody but Uncle Randolph had ever known that he was the pirate to them. When people had talked about the Morgans Robina had listened, and said, 'Good for him,' if it was something about improvements and profits at the works. She had met Leo Morgan a couple of times at parties in the last twelve months. He didn't socialise much, at least not locally, and neither did Robina these days. Both times they had exchanged a few words. Both times the prettiest girls there had flocked around him, he *was* the local tycoon, and Robina wasn't even sure he remembered who she was.

No, it wasn't odd that he didn't know how she felt about him, when no one else in the world did now, except perhaps Chris. But Leo Morgan was safe, she couldn't hurt him. Although if a chance arose she would find it hard to let it slip by.

Sarah was alone when Robina went back into the drawing room, and Robina said at once, 'It's settled—I stay.'

With a squeal of delight Sarah threw her arms around Robina's neck. 'I *am* glad, I am so *pleased*! You know, I'm almost glad now that he brought me back here.' Robina's eyebrows rose and Sarah grimaced, 'Well, almost.' Chris appeared in the doorway and Sarah announced triumphantly, 'She's going to stay here. Isn't that lovely?'

'You're sure?' Chris came across the room and as Sarah released Robina he put both hands on his sister's shoulders, looking into her face. She managed a smile for him, asking him,

'Don't you think it's a good idea.'

'Yes, I do.' There was a little colour in her cheeks, she had been so pale. She was looking more human, more alive, and he was glad about that because he loved her. 'I'd like you to come with me,' he said, 'but if you'd rather stay down here then I think it's the perfect answer.' His eyes met Sarah's. 'Thank you,' he said, and she said quickly,

'Don't thank me, I'll love having Robina staying.' She dimpled. 'Although I was rather clever, wasn't I, to think of it?'

'You certainly were,' Chris agreed, and sighed. 'Well, I can't put it off any longer. I have to be on my way.'

'Must you?' The protest broke from Robina, and he grinned ruefully at her. 'Afraid so. I just more or less walked out.' She hadn't thought about the upheaval that midnight summons must have caused. Chris was a vital part of the team and everything and everybody must have been thrown out of mesh. He had come as soon as he could, and he had stayed until the funeral, but now of course he had to get back.

'Sorry,' she said. 'Of course you must go.'

'I'll ring you when I reach town, and don't start worrying about a thing. I'll get in touch with somebody about——' he glanced across at the window. Across the bay was the Castle. Chris would see to things. Robina didn't even need to go over there.

'Come and see me off,' he said. He took her arm and they went out together to where his car was still standing in the drive, his case on the back seat. Sarah followed them, and at the door of the car Chris kissed Robina, ' 'Bye, Bina-baby, chin up.' He tilted her chin and she felt her eyes blur, as she watched him take both Sarah's hands and say, 'Thank you for everything. You're a treasure.'

'I know,' said Sarah. 'Have a good journey, and don't worry about us. We'll be just fine, you'll see.'

The lump hurt in Robina's throat, and she had to be alone, if it was only for a few minutes. She watched Chris's car turn, and vanish, and then she said huskily, 'Shall I change my room? If I'm staying you'll want me to move into something a bit smaller.'

'You stay where you are,' said Sarah, firmly, although it was probably one of the best guest rooms. Well, if they needed it, thought Robina, they could tell her. She said,

'Thank you. Would you mind if I went up for a little while? I'd like to get changed out of this.' She was in black, and that was a reasonable request, but Sarah looked quite distressed.

'Oh, *please*, you don't have to ask me what you can do. This is your home, you know, as though we were sisters. I always wanted a sister.'

'Did you?'

Sarah's lips curved. 'Two of us might be able to make a stand against my brother.' She was trying to make Robina smile, which was nice of her, but maybe the joke had a serious side. 'I'll be in the drawing room,' said Sarah.

Robina went to the bedroom that was hers now, because

for a little while at any rate this was her home. She hadn't thought clearly about her future yet. All she knew was that she was lonely, because Sarah for all her kindness wasn't her sister, and this companion business could just be a whim for her. She must have a will-o'-the-wisp personality, the way she had flitted from place to place, the number of men whose names had been linked with hers. In a few days she might decide that the last thing she wanted was a live-in 'sister'.

Uncle Randolph had been closer to Robina than anyone else, closer even than Chris because Chris's visits to the Castle had been few and far between, and it was over six months since Robina had been up to London to stay with him. She would miss Uncle Randolph every hour of the day.

She got out of her black suit and put on a thick blue jersey dress. There was a pile of condolence letters on the dressing table; Chris had opened and read them and told her who had sent them, and left them for her to see. These were from today's mail, there were more in a drawer and so far she hadn't read one. Perhaps she should have done while she was still in shock before it started to hurt so badly. Because when she picked up the first and read the first lines, tears spilled over, and she pushed the letters aside and let the tears flow, her face in her hands, sobbing soundlessly.

Even during these last months, when he was a broken man, Uncle Randolph had been her support. Robina had known that she could take her troubles to him and that he would have died for her. In a way he had. Losing him had left an empty place in her life and she couldn't see how it could ever be filled. She was on her own now, starting afresh in a strange room. She looked around with an interest she hadn't felt before, and it was a very attractive room, but if it was going to be her bedroom she would like to bring in a few personal things. Her old bedroom had been burned out, together with almost all her clothes. The cosmetics on this dressing table and the toiletries in the bathroom had either been given to her by Sarah or had been bought during the last few days. Even her handbag was new. Everything was new, including her life. There was hardly anything left from the old life except the shell of the Castle, a little furniture, and her abiding detestation of Leo Morgan.

She washed her face, and bathed her eyes to reduce the puffiness, then she made up skilfully. She hadn't bothered this week, she hadn't cared how she looked. She didn't much care now, but her pride was coming back and she wasn't going around looking a wreck in front of the pirate.

It was about half an hour later when Sarah looked in and said, 'Come and have a cup of tea.'

'All right.' Robina was still sitting at the dressing table, she had made herself take out the letters and she was reading them. Sarah came into the room and sat on the bed and said sympathetically,

'It's been a horrid day, hasn't it? The funeral and everything.'

'Yes, it has.'

'And your brother having to go.'

'Yes.'

'He's nice. You're lucky.'

'I am, yes.' She still had Chris, and not every girl had a brother like him, but Sarah said,

'So am I really. Lucky in having Leo.'

Robina put the letter back in its envelope. It was from a man who had worked with Uncle Randolph, recalling his kindness and generosity. But the man worked for Leo Morgan now and was probably taking home a pay packet that had trebled.

'There are lots of things we don't agree about,' said

Sarah, looking thoughtful, and watching her own reflection in the dressing table mirror. 'But he's super really.'

'Not over-protective?' said Robina quietly, and Sarah shrugged.

'Sometimes, but he's got me out of some scrapes in my time.' A shadow fell on her face. 'And through the worst one of all.' She probably meant her marriage. The man had been young and handsome, from a good family, a playboy who had never done a real day's work.

It had all happened long before Leo Morgan took over the Jefferson factory, but everyone knew how he had tried to stop them and how Sarah had eloped and married on her birthday. The romance had got plenty of publicity, and then, six months later, the young husband, high on drugs and alcohol, had crashed his car and killed both himself and his girl passenger. Before then the gossip writers had been listing the humiliations of Sarah, the public rows, the times her husband had left parties—and come to them—with somebody else. The marriage must have crumbled within weeks, but she had stayed around for those six months, and then her brother had fetched her and she had changed her name back to Morgan.

'I should have listened to him there,' she said, and her eyes on Robina were very steady. 'He's a rock, my brother.'

He probably was for Sarah. Captain Morgan probably took care of his crew, although he didn't give much quarter to outsiders.

'Welcome to the family,' he had just said to Robina, and now she was Sarah's surrogate sister. Did that mean he considered her his sister too? Maybe she was under Leo Morgan's protection now, but that didn't stop her hating his guts. Although settling in shouldn't be hard, because she really did like Sarah.

After tea, that first evening, they watched TV for a while, and then they listened to records, played in a music centre that was disguised as a piece of antique furniture.

Sarah's favourites were the hits of the moment, but there was a library of jazz, rock, country and Western and classical. Anyone who enjoyed any sort of music could surely find it here. The room was made for relaxing, panelled in pine, with a creamy all-over carpet and comfortable chairs and sofas. A fire burned in the fireplace and Robina thought, I'd settle for just this room, and a little bedroom and a kitchen. It would make a wonderful home, if only I could say who walks in through that door.

She would have been happy to have Sarah here, but the thought that Leo could put in an appearance any time was a nagging irritation. After the interview in his study she hadn't seen him again. She and Sarah had had a cup of tea, and later dined together. The food had been delicious, and although Robina had no appetite she had eaten. She had to stay strong, so she had to eat. They hadn't done much talking, Sarah had known this was a bad day for Robina; and they weren't doing much talking now, while the music was playing and they were both sitting in deep armchairs, Sarah curled into hers, Robina with her long slim legs crossed at the ankles, her hands clasped behind her head.

When the phone rang Sarah picked up an extension and said, 'Hello,' into it, then held it out to Robina. 'It's your brother.'

Robina had been waiting for Chris's call. She jumped up, hurrying. 'Hello? Chris? You got back all right?'

'Of course I did. And how are you? Settling in all right?'

'Very nicely.' She smiled at Sarah who was making no bones about listening, standing beside her.

'No troubles?' asked Chris.

'None.' Of course she was troubled, but grief was something she must handle herself.

'Good,' said Chris. 'That's the spirit. Laura here would like a word.'

'Hello,' said the husky voice of Chris's glamorous girl-friend. 'I can't tell you how sorry I am about everything. I never met him and I know there was this split with Chris chucking it all in and everything, but he must have been a super old man.'

'He was,' said Robina. He wasn't that old, for goodness' sake, but Laura who was Robina's age considered every-one over forty as ancient.

'And the castle getting burnt down,' she said ruefully, 'and I never saw that either.' She seemed to be classing Randolph Jefferson and Cliffe Castle together as things she had missed, but after a deep sigh she asked, 'Did Chris tell you my news?' in a brighter voice.

'No.'

'Oh well, I've got this fantastic part in a TV series.'

Robina said that was marvellous, and Laura told her all about the plot and the part, and Robina went on murmuring about how exciting it all sounded until Chris took the phone from Laura. 'This is costing a fortune,' he said. 'I'll call you again in a day or two. You're all right now? 'Bye, then.'

'That was his girl-friend,' Robina explained to Sarah. 'Her name's Laura Linsey. She's an actress, you might have seen her.' She described a play in which Laura had had a small part, and an advertisement in which she had appeared, but Sarah shook her head and asked, 'Is she beautiful?'

'Very.' Laura had dark red hair, smooth and long, and a face like a Barbie doll.

'And nice?' asked Sarah.

'I like her,' said Robina. 'She's always been nice to me and she seems to suit Chris.'

They had had wine with the dinner and brought their

glasses and the still half-full bottle in here with them. Sarah went back to her chair and picked up her glass and sipped a little. Then she said, 'So that's Chris's girl-friend. How about you? Do you have somebody special?'

'I've got friends, but nobody special.'

'Honestly?' Sarah sounded unconvinced. 'You mean not right now. With your looks there's got to be somebody.'

'Thank you,' said Robina. She had been told she was beautiful before, and when she'd looked at the portraits of long-ago Jefferson women she had seen her own face and known that she was a beauty. She had always attracted men wherever she went, but she hadn't gone far in recent years. The men who pursued her had found that she had very little time for them, the Castle was a round-the-clock job, and her affairs always seemed to peter out after a while.

'There's nobody special,' she said.

'Why not?'

Robina shrugged. 'I've never met anyone who mattered that much.' She had been happy enough with her life before the night of the storm. She hadn't wanted it changed. She said slowly, 'I don't think I've ever been in love. There's certainly never been a man I couldn't live without. How about you? How often have you been in love?'

Sarah had had a much more colourful career. In comparison Robina's past was dull as ditchwater. Let Sarah do the confessing if this was girl-talk time.

'Just once,' said Sarah, her smiling face stilled, and Robina knew that she was remembering the tragedy of her life. She must have loved the man she had married, and for all her gaiety and gadding since the memory lingered. Suddenly Robina felt closer to Sarah, and anxious that the future should be bright for the girl who seemed to have everything.

'To the future,' said Sarah, raising her glass, and Robina gasped,

'I was just thinking that. Hoping for the best, for both of us.'

'You won't be so busy now,' said Sarah. 'You'll have time to look around for somebody special.'

It sounded fine, but there could be danger in having time on her hands and being lonely for the first time. She mustn't start desperately searching for love just to have someone close. 'What's he got to be like?' Sarah was smiling again, her eyes dancing, and Robina laughed,

'What are you suggesting I do? Make out a list and send it to one of these computer dating set-ups?'

'Hey, why not?' Sarah chortled. 'I never thought about that. But you won't need a computer, you'll find him soon enough. I just wondered what kind of man turns you on.'

Robina's mind ran backwards like a film being played at speed, faces flashing at her briefly. She had liked some of her admirers very much, but in the end she had always let them go or sent them on their way. Not one of them had turned her on, as Sarah meant it. She grinned, 'Maybe I'm frigid, but I can't think of any particular type that would bowl me over on sight.'

Sarah's eyebrows went first down then up, considering this. Then she grinned too and said, 'Don't give me that frigid guff, but you are a very cool lady.'

Sarah thought this was reserve on Robina's part, a refusal to discuss love affairs and lovers, but if Robina had had an ideal man she wouldn't have minded describing him for Sarah. Only she hadn't.

Among the men who had fancied her there had never been one whose caresses had stirred more than a brief surface pleasure. She hadn't lost herself for a moment in anyone's arms, and now she had nobody to run to if things went wrong—except Chris, and he was far away living his own life—maybe it would be as well if she stayed cool.

Sarah put on more records and Robina, listening to them,

wondered what her thoughts were, because most of the
love songs seemed to be about unhappiness. But Sarah
smiled when she caught Robina's eye and said, 'I think we
should go shopping tomorrow.'

'Yes, all right.'

'To get you some clothes. You're going to need all sorts
of things.'

She didn't have all sorts of things. She hadn't had much
for years and she had less than ever since the fire, but she
said cautiously, 'I don't want to go mad, I have to be careful, I'm very short of cash.'

'I've a charge account,' said Sarah airily. 'We're having
a dinner party on Friday, you'll need a new dress for that
for a start.'

It wasn't Sarah's money or Robina might have accepted,
on the basis of a loan. Leo Morgan might give his sister
everything she asked for, but the cash was his.

A salary was different. You earned a salary, but Robina
wanted nothing from Leo Morgan that smacked of charity.
She said, 'I'd rather buy my own clothes. I think I can run
to an evening dress.' But when Sarah's face clouded she
felt petty and apologised, 'Sorry. It's sweet of you, but I
just can't put my things on your account.'

'Why not?' Sarah wasn't used to being crossed. She
pouted prettily. 'It would be fun, and you did lose practically all your wardrobe and those few things you bought
were dreary. I was looking forward to having a lovely
splurge.'

It would be lovely. Robina had lived mainly in jeans and
tops, with skirts for best, but she could remember having
beautiful clothes, and missed them. She hadn't realised
how much till now, when she looked at Sarah in her model
suit and felt 'dreary' in her own rather shapeless dress.
Sarah was right there. She hadn't cared what she'd bought

the last time they went shopping, but she could have done better than this. 'All right,' she said, 'I'll get some things, but only what I can afford.'

'Oh, *Robina*!' Sarah was exasperated. 'Don't be so stubborn!' She shook her head, as though she was chiding a wilful child. 'Robina's an awful mouthful,' she said. 'Can I call you Bina, like your brother does?'

'If you like. It's a long time since anyone did. Not since I was a baby. Chris doesn't usually.'

'Well, I shall,' Sarah decided, and her mood changed. She didn't argue any more. They just went on listening to the records and sipping their wine, and Sarah talked about the folk who would be coming to the dinner party: a lawyer, a Public Relations man, a girl who designed textiles, and a couple whom Robina knew slightly.

It was not far off midnight when they heard a car and Sarah who was putting on another record announced, 'That's Leo.' If he came in here the peace would be shattered for Robina, but she could hardly scuttle away, although she wished now that she had started yawning earlier and asked if Sarah would mind if she went up to bed.

He did come in. He smiled at both of them, then sat down and said, 'Do you like this stuff?'

Somebody on the record sounded as though he was being strangled to an accompaniment of crashing tin trays, and Robina had to admit, 'It's the first time I've heard it.'

'With luck it'll be the last,' said Leo.

'Do you mind!' protested Sarah. 'That's a friend of mine singing. That was a prezzie.'

'He'll have to give them away,' said Leo. 'He'll never sell 'em.'

'You look tired,' Sarah said abruptly, and Robina felt a pang because she had said that so often to Uncle Randolph. She had imagined the pirate was tireless, but of course nobody was. The lines were deep around his eyes and cutting from nose to mouth, and Sarah hovered, demanding, 'Have you eaten?'

'Yes.' She seemed older and more mature in her concern for her brother. Although he looked strong as a bull to Robina, as though he could go without food or sleep for days and recover after one good meal and eight hours' rest. 'It's been a long day,' he said, 'for all of us.' He looked at Robina. Presumably he had been working since, but he had been at the funeral and—damn him—he was sorry for her. 'You should be getting some rest,' he told her.

'We waited for you,' said Sarah. 'Well, I did. I want you to settle something for me.' This must be a familiar routine, thought Robina. 'We're going shopping tomorrow,' Sarah went on. 'Bina needs some clothes.'

'Bina?' Leo echoed.

'Short for——'

'So I gathered.'

Robina was stiff and silent. She didn't want him using her pet name, she would have preferred to be Miss Jefferson to him. But there was nothing she could do or say, and she knew now that Sarah had given up the argument until she could bring in the big guns.

'She's got to buy clothes, hasn't she?' Sarah was putting the case to Leo. 'She's got hardly anything left from the fire and she'll be needing all sorts of things.' Robina felt a hot indignant blush rising. 'A dress for Friday night for a start,' Sarah went on, 'and I say she should charge it on my account, but she's insisting that she'll be paying for everything herself.'

'Would you have bought an evening dress tomorrow,' he asked Robina, 'if you hadn't taken on the job as companion to this one?'

Of course she wouldn't. She shook her head and he said, 'Then it obviously goes with the job. By the way, you should be getting your first month's salary.' He wrote out the cheque, and he knew that she was probably broke. Her affairs were in such a tangle. She needed this cheque to get her through the next four weeks, and she was lucky to have a roof over her head and have meals guaranteed. The lunacy of it suddenly struck her, arguing over the price of a dress. She certainly couldn't afford the luxury of pride. If clothes were part of the job then they were a uniform and she'd accept them. She said, 'Thank you,' and picked up the cheque, and Sarah yawned.

'Ready for bed, now that's settled?'

On their way upstairs Robina said, 'You shouldn't have done that. Getting your brother in on the argument.'

'The end justifies the means,' Sarah quoted smugly, and when Robina stared at her, 'Haven't you heard the saying?'

'Oh yes, I've heard it,' said Robina. 'But you sound as if you believe it.'

Sarah dimpled. 'Sometimes,' she said, and when they reached the door of Robina's room she kissed her cheek lightly. 'Have a good night's rest now. And it is going to be all right. You know, that future we were talking about.'

'Of course it is,' said Robina. Life stretched ahead golden with promise for Sarah, but her own future was shadowed with uncertainty and the dark presence of Leo Morgan.

She slept sounder than she had expected. 'Breakfast around ten,' Sarah had said, and this would be the first morning Robina had taken herself downstairs. She felt no happier than she had on those other mornings in this house, but she was more herself. She had accepted her bereavement, and it was good to have something to do. That cheque, with Leo Morgan's signature written with a broad nib in black ink, had to be earned, although she couldn't imagine Sarah being an over-demanding employer.

Mrs Palmer the housekeeper greeted her at the bottom of the stairs. Jack Palmer was the gardener, a chauffeur

and a daily help made up the staff, and this was the first
time Robina had seen Mrs Palmer clearly. She and her
husband had come here with Leo Morgan, but Robina had
never met either of them until the night of the fire, and she
had hardly noticed who was around her during the days
that followed.

Now she smiled at the trim middle-aged woman carrying an empty tray across the hall, and Mrs Palmer said,
'Good morning, miss, are you feeling better?' It was as
though Robina was convalescent after an illness. She had
had everyone's sympathy, the double tragedy of losing her
uncle and her home had shocked them all, and when Robina
said now, 'Yes thank you,' Mrs Palmer thought that was a
good sign. She hadn't seen Robina smile before. 'I've just
taken the papers in,' she said encouragingly, 'and some
more coffee.'

As it was only just after eight o'clock and Sarah didn't
breakfast until ten Robina should have known that Leo had
to be at the table, but seeing him sitting there rocked her
on her feet. She was at the door of the breakfast room and
it was too late to back out without a word, so she had to
say, 'Good morning.'

She had been right about his rate of recuperation; there
was no sign of weariness about him this morning. He
looked relaxed and refreshed in body and mind, more than
able to deal with any problems the day might bring.
'Coffee?' he asked.

'Er—no, thanks. I—thought I'd take a walk round the
garden.'

He had reached the toast and marmalade stage. A couple
of folded newspapers were beside his plate and several
letters, and he was pouring coffee into a big cup. She would
have liked some, but not if it meant sitting here and drinking it.

'Are you fond of gardening?' he asked her.

She didn't stammer this time, telling him, 'I did most of it. Well, it was just mowing lawns and a very small vegetable garden patch. They used to be beautiful gardens.'

'I can imagine,' he said. Before he came the money had stopped coming in, and all but a small and changing staff had gone, but they had still been happy—she and Uncle Randolph—until the pirate took over their lives.

'As your gardens will be,' she said. 'Very soon.'

They had only been planted a year ago, but already shrubs and plants were flowering, hedges and trees had taken root. Old trees, standing here already, had been incorporated into the design and in another few years this was going to pass for a mature garden, while the Castle grounds would probably run wild.

'I hope so.' Leo picked up the top letter and because he frowned at it Robina's attention was caught. It was an airmail and he was scowling. She waited for him to open it, although it couldn't possibly be any business of hers, with a quickening delight because something was annoying him. But he looked up at her and then she had to turn away.

She went out into the gardens, and talked knowledgeably about gardening for a while with a man she found working there. The day was fine as she strolled around, rarely glancing across at the Castle, although there was still that illusion that the lightning strike had caused very little damage. How easy it had been to become accepted in this house, so that the pirate would have poured coffee for her and opened his mail in front of her, even the letter that had brought his black brows together.

It was too late now to tell Uncle Randolph that Leo Morgan had weaknesses, that he came home weary sometimes and some letters started his day badly. But that airmail letter had given a good start to her day, it had made her feel good. She stood on the smooth turf of the newly laid lawns, looking across at the green sweep in front of the

Castle, where her uncle had wept when Leo Morgan told him he was of no value, and where, a week ago, he had died. Seeing Morgan with that letter had been as sweet as a little taste of revenge, and she knew that she would watch and listen and search for some way she could harm him. It couldn't help Uncle Randolph now, but it might be the only way she could free herself from this corroding bitterness.

CHAPTER THREE

ROBINA stayed outside in the gardens until she heard the
crunch of car wheels on the gravel and saw the big black
car going up the hillside. Then she went into the break-
fastroom. Mrs Palmer, clearing the table, asked her, 'Ready
for breakfast, miss?' and she said, 'I'll wait for Sarah.'

'Just as you like. Can I get you some tea or coffee?'

'Coffee would be lovely.'

The two newspapers were still there, and there were a
couple of letters. Both were addressed to Sarah, one was
the airmail, although Robina was almost certain that Leo
Morgan had been about to open that. The way he was holding it was the way you did hold an envelope to tear it, only
he had looked up and Robina had been watching and maybe that had changed his mind.

The stamps were Spanish and although there was no
name or address on the back she was pretty sure this was
from Sarah's fisherman. Leo had looked thunderous when
he'd picked it up, so he must have recognised the postmark
or the writing, and Sarah's recent affair had caused him a
fair amount of inconvenience. He had disapproved and he
had got her away, and he wouldn't be keen on love letters
following her. It was a small world for girls like Sarah
Morgan, who could hop on a jet any time.

Robina sipped her coffee and thought, I wouldn't mind
being the one to tell your brother you'd gone back to
what's-his-name. Leo was worse than a Victorian father.
Sarah was twenty-one years old, she had been married, she
had been around. Surely she didn't need this kind of
chauvinistic domination.

I wouldn't stand for it, Robina thought; and a smile tugged her lips at the thought of Chris laying down the law, vetting her friends. Chris would advise her if she asked for advice, but he would never in a million years break up a relationship which was making her happy. Chris believed in happiness, but Leo Morgan believed in safety. Safety for Sarah that was; he must take risks galore himself.

Robina had read one newspaper and was half way through the second before Sarah put in an appearance. She beamed at Robina, 'Hello, been down long?' and pounced on her letters.

Robina watched as Sarah read, and saw the smile, sweet and secretive, as though someone was whispering the words in Sarah's ear. When Sarah slipped the letter into her pocket Robina said, 'Your brother saw it. I think he was in two minds whether to open it, only I was standing around. He didn't seem too pleased.'

'He wouldn't have learned much if he had read it,' said Sarah cheerfully, but it had told her all she needed to know. She had her smug look again, as though things were going right for Sarah, and Robina wondered if they had a code so that apparently innocuous phrases had a hidden meaning.

Sarah was obviously waiting for another question, so Robina asked the obvious. 'It's from your Spanish friend, of course?'

'Carlos.'

'You're still fond of him?'

'I might be.' Sarah sat down and began to pour coffee, and Robina demanded,

'Then why did you let your brother bring you back here? You're not a child. Why should he order your life for you?'

Sarah was wearing a silk negligee in ice blue that made her skin look warm and peachlike. It was frilly, frothy, impractical and very expensive. She had brought a wave of pricy perfume into the room with her, and from the crown of her shining blonde head to the soft kid sandals on her feet she looked rich and pampered. 'Because I'm not cut out to be marrying a poor man,' she said. 'Not unless Leo keeps up my allowance.'

But she and her Spanish lover were still in touch, and that hadn't pleased Leo Morgan. Robina warned her, 'Well, I should stop him writing here if I were you, even if you have got your own code going.' Sarah's grin admitted it. 'Unless you get up in time to grab the mail before your brother gets it,' then she added, 'Or I will if you like.'

'Would you?' said Sarah. 'Thank you, I really appreciate that. But I don't get many letters from him, just one occasionally so that Leo can see they're few and far between.'

'Oh?' So what was going on?

'There is such a thing as a telephone service, you know,' said Sarah, and Robina almost choked on her coffee. That was so obvious that Leo Morgan must appreciate the risk, but he couldn't do a thing. He'd have no check at all if Sarah didn't phone from home or get her calls here. Whether the affair was serious or not it was nice to know that they were pulling the wool over his eyes.

'What's he like?' Robina asked, and Sarah's eyes shone.

'Oh, fantastically handsome. Dark curly hair, tall.' She breathed deeply, savouring memories. 'Exciting. A bit of a devil.'

I shouldn't like you to get hurt, thought Robina, but I'd love this dark-eyed devil of yours to come back at the pirate. She said, 'Good luck,' and Sarah who was opening her second envelope, which contained a fashion circular, put it down and reached across to touch Robina's hand.

'You really mean that, don't you?' There was almost a catch in Sarah's voice, and her face was suddenly serious. 'You really do wish us luck.'

'Of course.' She wished Sarah good luck, but her heart's

desire was that Leo Morgan should strike a patch of luck so appalling that it would make him sick of living.

'I'm so glad you feel that way,' said Sarah. 'I might need help some time.'

'Anything,' said Robina. It looked as though getting her own back on the pirate was going to be easy, but she found it hard to meet Sarah's eyes, and she was glad that the subject of Carlos seemed to be closed for the time being.

'I'm ravenous,' said Sarah. 'Be a sweetie and press the button, will you?' She looked across towards the fireplace and Robina got up and summoned Mrs Palmer.

Being waited on was a new experience for Robina. She was used to cooking, and clearing up afterwards, but Sarah took service for granted. After breakfast they went upstairs, and Sarah selected her day's outfit from a wardrobe that filled the whole of one of her bedroom walls. Everything had a couture name, and Robina could see what a sacrifice it would be for Sarah to risk all this by marrying or living with a man against her brother's wishes.

It was blackmail, but unless Sarah fell madly in love, or unless she could persuade Leo to go on paying her allowance, she would probably settle for her secret lover.

Pity, thought Robina, as Sarah slipped into a Jean Muir dress, because she couldn't see herself betraying a confidence and 'shopping' Sarah for the satisfaction of sending up Leo Morgan's blood pressure.

Robina had a Mini. Uncle Randolph's Daimler, a company car, had gone with the company, and Robina's little bus had seen better days. But it had come unscathed through the fire. It was kept in the coach house and that hadn't burned, and Chris had brought it over here for her. It was in the garage now, but well back, and Sarah produced the keys to her gleaming maroon sports car without giving the Mini a glance.

'Wouldn't you like to drive?' she offered.

'Oh, my gosh!' Robina took a backwards step. 'I'd be scared to death!'

'Don't you like driving?'

'I love it, but that is some car. Suppose I got into an argument with a wall or something?'

'What's insurance for?' said Sarah. 'Besides, I'm not that keen on driving and if I get Tom to taxi me around he's probably spying for Leo.' The chauffeur who was under the bonnet of a Lotus standing alongside the sports car chuckled, and Sarah said, 'He thinks I think he thinks I'm joking.'

The chauffeur was a small wiry man with a lined face and sharp eyes. He came out smiling and Sarah was laughing, but Robina wondered whether there was some truth in what she had said. Tom was Leo Morgan's man, just as the Palmers were in his pay and his service, and it was quite possible that they shared his concern for Sarah. She wondered if Mrs Palmer had looked twice at that airmail before she had taken it into the breakfast room and if she would tell her husband, 'There was one from Spain for her. The master wouldn't like that.'

'You're not driving, then?' said Sarah, opening the door on the driver's side.

'I'd love to,' Robina stroked the wheel longingly, 'but I couldn't just get in and drive off. I daren't take that kind of chance with this kind of car.'

She had driven cars that Chris had bought. He was always changing his car. But he went in for secondhand 'bargains' and she wasn't worried about anything that belonged to Chris, the way she would have been embarrassed if she had so much as scratched Leo Morgan's property.

'Would you like a little tuition, miss?' the chauffeur suggested, and Robina was delighted.

'That *is* kind of you. Oh, I would!'

'Right,' said Sarah. 'We've got to be off now, but if you're around when we get back, Tom.'

'I'll be here, miss,' said Tom.

Sarah was an average driver; Robina felt safe enough beside her as they took the coast road heading for a larger town, twenty miles away. It was a pleasure, sitting back in the smooth-running car, listening to the radio and to Sarah's continual chatter.

Robina concentrated on listening to Sarah because that stopped her thinking about Uncle Randolph. It would have been easy to start crying, to get choked up, but she was being paid to take this trip, and to be cheerful company, so she gave all her attention to the things that Sarah was saying.

You had to like Sarah. If Robina had been less resentful when Sarah came calling at the Castle she would have liked her then, because—apart from being so pretty—she was fun. She bubbled with good humour, and she could gleefully tell a story against herself.

She made Robina laugh when she described the time when Leo had agreed to let her appear in a TV advert for one of his companies. 'I fancied that,' she said. 'I thought, This is it, I'll never be Leo Morgan's sister again, I'll be Sarah Morgan, model.' She pealed with laughter. 'You should have seen the tests, I was *awful*! I sounded as though I'd got a hot potato in my mouth and I looked like somebody with mumps.' She had given it such a build-up that Robina had expected to hear that the advert starring Sarah would be appearing soon. She was astonished that Sarah had flopped. 'They couldn't get me out quick enough,' Sarah giggled. 'Leo bought me a super ring as a consolation prize and I went off to Spain to get over the shock.'

'And met Carlos?'

'I'd known Carlos for ages. We've had the villa for years and his family have been there for ever. But this was the holiday it all happened.'

'I can't believe it,' said Robina. 'I should have thought you'd have looked wonderful. You're prettier than Chris's Laura and she's a successful model.'

'Am I?' Sarah sounded pleased. She peeked at herself in the driving mirror, then giggled again. 'Well, I surely didn't film like a model, although I don't photograph too badly. Funny, that. I'll bet you photograph fantastically, with your cheekbones.'

Robina remembered the paintings of the women with her face and wondered if any were left. In the main hall and half way up the staircase there had been two, with a hundred years between them: a Regency beauty and an Edwardian hostess. She remembered the flames as she and Uncle Randolph stumbled down the stairs, and she could almost see her Edwardian great-great-grandmother with the high-piled hair and the low-cut dress, and the collar of three rows of perfectly matched pearls. Then the face blackened and crumbled, and Robina shivered.

'Once we've got you some decent clothes,' said Sarah, 'you're going to look stunning. And you'll need a session at the beauty salon.'

Robina knew that, dressed like Sarah, she would be turning heads as easily as Sarah did. Sarah was kind, but not many girls were anxious to bring out the sex appeal of other women, and Robina said, 'I can understand that you don't want your companion looking a drag, but why am I getting a beauty treatment?'

'I'm going there this afternoon,' said Sarah. 'You might as well. They can fit you in.'

'Lovely, but why?'

They were stationary at traffic lights and Sarah turned her wide candid gaze on Robina. 'This dinner party on

Friday, I told you about Bernard?' That he was a lawyer in his thirties, successful and stodgy. 'Well, he's one of the men Leo thinks would make me a good husband, and I'd like him talking to you as well as to me, because he bores me stiff.'

Robina gasped, then laughed. 'That's very nice! If I start monopolising your brother's friends I'm going to get the sack before my first week's out.'

'You don't have to monopolise him,' said Sarah, as the lights changed and she jammed her foot down and the car shot away like a racehorse from the trap. 'You don't even have to take much notice of him. I can do with somebody to take his eye off me, that's all.'

'What about the textile designer?' From Sarah's earlier description she was young and elegant and striking, but Sarah shrugged and her mouth turned down.

'Imogen won't be looking at anyone but Leo.'

'She and Leo belong together, do they?' Robina was trying to follow the ramifications of the Morgan household, and Sarah overtook a couple of cyclists and a bus before she answered.

'She's working on it, but so far it's only a sleeping partnership.'

Robina had led a quiet life for a long time, and she was beginning to look forward to Friday. She knew two of the guests, a local estate agent and his wife, but the rest would be new faces. The lawyer who was supposed to make Sarah forget her handsome Spaniard, and the girl who was having an affair with Leo Morgan, sounded an unlucky pair, but it would be interesting to see them, and very pleasant to wear a new dress and have her hair professionally styled.

'Here we are,' said Sarah, nodding at a shop fronted with large flat Georgian bow windows in which Robina caught a glimpse of beautiful clothes. 'The car park's round the back.'

Everyone knew Miss Morgan. She had a cluster of assistants around her, all smiling, before she had taken more than half a dozen steps into the shop. There was a private room and they were ushered into it like royalty.

The proprietor greeted them, jumping up from behind a white and gold desk. She was an angular woman, in a neat hairstyle and a neat suit, and she looked as though Sarah's arrival had made her day. 'How *lovely* to see you,' she said, 'I'm so glad you dropped in. I was thinking of phoning you, we've just got some really lovely things in,' and when Sarah explained that they were shopping for her friend, not herself, that was no problem at all.

Evening dresses were brought out and Robina tried on the ones that Sarah liked best. She would have settled for any that fitted her, they were all much prettier and pricier than anything that had been in her wardrobe for years. Given her choice she would have picked a scarlet chiffon, because the colour was so gorgeous, but Sarah was going for the muted shades and it was on Sarah's account, and this was how Sarah wanted her companion to look.

When Robina put on the gown of oyster silk Sarah said, 'Oh yes!' and Robina looked at herself in the long mirror. The dress had style. It was simple, flowing smoothly over her firm young breasts, spanning her narrow waist. The sleeves were long and the neck was high, and when she moved it swished very softly.

'Do you like it?' asked Sarah.

'It's beautiful. How much——?'

'We'll take it,' said Sarah. 'Now you need a suit.'

Robina hardly said a word. Sarah was doing all the talking, and the proprietor and her staff must have wondered at Robina's attitude until someone addressed her as, 'Miss—er?' and she said, 'Jefferson.'

Then they realised who she was. They knew about the fire at the Castle, there had been a photograph of Robina in several newspapers. The Morgans were neighbours and Sarah Morgan was obviously helping a friend in trouble.

After that the smiles became sympathetic and Robina was treated very gently. She let Sarah get on with it. She tried on the clothes that were brought for her. She daren't think how the bill was totting up, but if she was going around with Sarah she would need a basic wardrobe of good clothes. And why not? Leo Morgan had made money out of her family, the business was flourishing now, like Uncle Randolph said he had got a bargain. So why should she worry about being an expense on him?

But she blinked when she saw it all being packed into boxes. Sarah was quite blasé, this was nothing unusual for her, but the pirate might quibble when he got the bill. In that case, someone would have to return them, but it wouldn't be Robina, although she wouldn't be wearing any of it until it got clearance.

'We'll call back and collect everything about three o'clock,' said Sarah.

They were booked in for the full treatment at the beauty salon, and Robina stripped down to her pants in the massage parlour and stretched out on the couch. Now she was here she was going to relax and enjoy it. She closed her eyes and the warm oils and the rhythmical moving fingertips of the masseuse unknotted the tensions so that she was soon drifting into a daydream of lying on a sunny beach where the hands that oiled her didn't belong to the girl in the white coat but to a man who was on holiday with her.

This wasn't a professional massage, it was a caressing interlude, and afterwards they would swim together in a blue sea, and after that they would go up to a little room, and the man was her lover, of course.

She wondered if Sarah was remembering her fisherman, and felt a stab of loneliness because all she had herself was a dream lover. She would find somebody, probably, before long. Two of those letters of condolence had come from men who had once told her they loved her. One was married now, his wife had signed it too, but the other wasn't and he had asked if he might see her again. On Friday night there would be this lawyer, who bored Sarah but might not bore Robina, who quite liked serious men. He might be very likeable, and in that gorgeous dress she would be worth looking at herself. If he fell for her that would annoy Leo and amuse Sarah.

She wondered what he looked like, and tried to imagine him, but somehow the dark menacing face of Leo Morgan came suddenly into her mind, jerking her head back as though he was literally bending over her. 'Anything the matter?' the startled masseuse asked anxiously, and Robina gave a wry little grin.

'Sorry—I was nearly asleep.'

In the end they didn't change her hairstyle. There was a conference about it, with books being consulted, and sketchy styles pinned in to see if it would be better shorter or smoother or different. But when it was combed out she still had her cloud of dark hair, with a special sheen on it now, and waves looking lusher and deeper.

They lunched at the beauty bar in the basement of the salon, on a variety of salads and fresh fruit, and every time Robina glimpsed herself in one of the mirrors she got a pleasant little glow. The professional make-up did wonders. The bone structure of her face was cleverly emphasised, the eye-shadow was exactly right, and Sarah's first reaction of 'Wow!' was rather how Robina felt herself.

There seemed to be no envy in Sarah at all. She seemed genuinely thrilled that Robina had been turned into a raving beauty, and sitting on a high stool at the buffet bar she looked as self-satisfied as an artist who has created a masterpiece.

'We're going to a nightclub tonight,' she announced,

'with a few friends. Dancing and that. You'll be a sensation.'

'Oh!' The prospect of a nightclub, all noise and frenzied gaiety, struck a sour note for Robina. She wanted to meet new people, but in a quiet fashion for a while. She said hesitantly, 'Do you think—would you mind if I didn't? I don't feel up to nightclubbing yet.'

'No?' Sarah frowned and looked thoughtful. 'No, I suppose it is too soon. I suppose you would rather have a quiet evening at home.' She smiled. 'You do whatever you want. I told you, we're sisters, that's how it's going to be.'

'You're a very nice girl,' said Robina gratefully. 'I hope I'll be some use to you as a companion. I promise I'll try to be useful,' and Sarah dimpled.

'You learn to drive my car,' she said. 'And then we'll be able to get around. I'm no good at long-distance driving, I get spots in front of my eyes after the first hour or so.'

Tom was waiting when they got back. Robina's parcels were stacked in Sarah's room, and Robina hurried downstairs and out again to where the car had been left in front of the garages. The chauffeur, who had greeted them ten minutes earlier was flicking dust off the gleaming dark red bonnet. 'Ready, miss?' he asked.

'Oh yes, please.'

She was looking forward to this. It was going to be a treat, and no danger with a professional driver beside her. She liked cars, she loved driving. But he seemed a trifle uncertain so that she asked, 'Anything wrong?'

He went on looking at her. 'Just something a bit different about you. You've got some colour in your cheeks, it's being out in the fresh air.' Robina stifled a smile. The difference was three hours in the beauty salon, extending from top to toe; even her toenails were now painted like pink pearls. 'You're looking healthier,' he decided, and having settled that, 'Now, miss, you do drive, of course. What kind of cars have you driven?'

She checked them off for him. 'My Mini, I've had that for nearly five years; and I did drive my uncle's, which was a Daimler. And my brother's, from when I was sixteen. They were sports cars, and the one he's got now, I've driven that—rather a clapped-out old Jag.'

Tom was nodding. Variety was satisfactory, it showed that the girl was an adaptable driver. He opened the door and invited her to, 'Get the feel of the wheel while I'll explain the controls to you.'

Robina listened closely. When he had finished she repeated what he had told her, and he was glad to find that she had absorbed and understood. It looked as though she was going to be an easier pupil than Miss Sarah, and probably a safer driver.

'Start 'er up,' he said, and the next fifteen minutes confirmed his snap judgment. Robina took it slowly at first, but she had a smooth touch, and after they had circled the area fronting the garage and outhouses, and done a few manoeuvres, he had no hesitation in letting her take the car up the drive and on to the road.

There was a fair amount of traffic, going both ways, but she would have passed a test if she had been taking one. She passed Tom's test. He liked the way she handled the controls without hesitation and her delight in the car. 'You're a natural, miss,' he told her.

'Thank you.' She overtook, safely, at the right speed. 'It's a beautiful car. How far can we go?'

'Round the town?' he suggested.

She knew the traffic lanes and the one-way streets. A turn round the town would be very good practice. 'I'd like that,' she said, and everything went perfectly. The car was a dream; it did just what she wanted it to do. If Sarah pre-

ferred the passenger seat she need never touch this wheel
again. Robina would be delighted to chauffeur her anywhere.

Goodness knows there wasn't much similarity between
this car and Robina's ancient Mini, but for years in her
Mini she had slowed down, on this stretch of road, driving
back from town. Just ahead was the entrance to the Castle.
She hadn't even glanced at it on her way out, she had
kept her eyes on the road, but now she was more relaxed
and instinctively she did what she had always done, slowed
down.

'Turning left, miss?' asked Tom.

She bit her lip and then said, 'Yes,' giving the signal.
She had to turn down here some time, and she would probably never feel better than she did now. She would just
drive round to the front, and look, before her reluctance to
return had time to harden into a pathological state. She
didn't even need to get out of the car. Just take it down
the drive that ran between trees out to the front of the
house that overlooked the sea, so that she could say to herself, 'I went back, I can go back again.'

She didn't turn her head. She knew every tree, and she
knew which windows she was passing, but she didn't look
up at them. She rounded the Castle heading towards the
coach house and stable block. Then when she came level
with the main door, she stopped—carefully, putting on the
handbrake and switching off the ignition.

Tom hadn't spoken since they left the road, but now she
heard the indrawn breath whistling between his teeth, and
she raised her head and looked. The grey stone mass of
the Castle was intact, but the wooden doors into the great
hall had gone. There were two planks of wood nailed across
and lettered in scarlet 'Danger, Keep Out', and beyond was
blackness. Through the high windows was the sky, and
the smell of burning still lingered—in her mind probably,

at the back of her throat so that she almost retched on it.
Everywhere was deathly quiet, except for a rustling that
might have been the leaves in the trees, but seemed to come
from the dead house where there was nothing but darkness
and echoes.

The cold was deep inside her as she reached to start up
the car again.

The chauffeur watched her, but her hand seemed steady,
she did a perfect three-point turn, and he reckoned she was
safe to go on driving.

There were tears in her eyes, but she blinked on them
fiercely, and knew exactly what she was doing. She was
driving with every care, not recklessly at all, getting away
from this place because there was nothing left. The Castle
was dead, and all her past had gone with it, everything she
loved had gone. Like Uncle Randolph. There was only
darkness left and echoes.

She slowed down, approaching the end of the drive, and
then somehow her foot slipped, and instead of stopping the
car shot forward, half way across the road, squealing as she
rammed on the brakes.

It could have caused carnage, but it coincided with a
break in the traffic, although the next few seconds were
chaotic.

Cars skidded and swerved, horns blared, drivers cursed.
It was like a nightmare dodgems, as Tom seized the wheel
and got them straightened out and then on to the grass
verge where they stopped. Miraculously there was no
sound of crashing cars, although as the traffic got back into
lanes the air rang with a chorus of furious male voices giving their opinion on bloody women drivers.

The chauffeur mopped his grey face and Robina put
her face in her hands. She had never had a miss as near as
that before. She had never had an accident before, and the
enormity of someone shooting straight across a busy road

appalled her. What she could have *done*! 'Thank God,' she whispered, and Tom muttered something that sounded like a prayer. He was looking through the back window where a car had drawn up behind, and Robina wasn't surprised. She saw it in the driving mirror and closed her eyes and let Tom get out to deal with it. Someone was going to ask if she thought she ought to be let loose on the roads, and right now she did not.

'What the hell is going on?' she heard Leo Morgan shout, and she opened her door and said, 'It was my fault. I came out of the drive too fast.'

'You can say that again!' His swarthy complexion was bloodless, he must have recognised the car and thought Sarah was in it. He looked into the car and then at her and asked, 'Are you all right?'

'Yes.' So was everyone else, but she could have caused a pile-up for miles. Whatever happened next she was so thankful.

'What were you doing at the wheel?' he demanded.

'Sarah wanted me to drive the car. I was having a lesson, but this was entirely my fault.'

Tom coughed, and said, 'She's a very good driver. She got in and handled it like an expert.'

'Experts don't come out of blind exits at forty miles an hour.' Leo retorted drily, and Robina couldn't have agreed more.

'I'm sorry. I hadn't been back to the Castle since——' Her tongue flicked between stiff lips. 'I didn't realise there was nothing. Across the bay it doesn't look too bad, but it's like a great tomb.' The traffic was moving normally now, although everybody who went past stared at them, and Leo Morgan stared at her too. Then he said. 'You think she's a good driver?' asking Tom with his eyes on Robina.

'Safer than Miss Sarah,' said Tom emphatically. 'And this isn't going to happen again.'

'You take my car.'

Tom saluted with a jaunty flip of the hand. 'Yes, sir.'

'And you,' said Leo, 'can drive me home.'

'Me?' Robina squeaked.

'It's the best way,' he answered her. 'Like getting back on the horse.'

He was right, and as it was his property she had nearly smashed this was more than decent of him, especially sitting beside her while she tried to get her nerve back. She knew she could drive the car and that was what she had to do. She couldn't waste any nervous energy on antipathy for the man who was getting into the passenger seat.

She breathed deeply and tried not to touch him, which wasn't easy because he was so big. She waited a few seconds, then drew out into the traffic and took the car home to the white house. The garage doors were open, and Tom was standing outside looking apprehensive, but as Robina came to a quiet halt he grinned, and Leo said,

'Good. Yes, that's fine.'

'I've never had an accident,' she said, 'and I've been driving since I was sixteen.' Her Mini lurked in the shadows at the back of the garage. 'That mostly,' she added, talking to herself. 'I must take care of that. It's about the only thing left.'

'You know there's furniture in the stables, of course?'

She looked blank for a moment; Chris had told her, but she had forgotten when she saw the Castle. She wondered what could have been saved from the holocaust, and said, 'So there is. My brother's arranging to get it valued, and sold, I suppose.'

She wanted to get out of the car, but it was difficult while he was sitting there talking. 'Your brother's in London, isn't he? Would you like me to——'

'*No!*' It would be too much to have Leo Morgan raking over the ashes of Cliffe Castle. 'No, thank you,' she said, because that first no had come out with an insulting fervour, and he smiled.

'Well, if you should need any help.'

Robina said, 'Thank you' again, and thought, There's no one in the world I would be less likely to ask. If we were the last two alive I'd manage on my own.

The door opened on her side and she hadn't realised that her back was pressed against it, keeping as much distance as she could between them, until she nearly fell out and Sarah caught her. 'Whoops!' exclaimed Sarah as Robina scrambled to her feet. 'What's this, then? A bit of trouble, Tom says. Don't tell me you ran into Leo. That wasn't very clever.'

Leo moved into the driving seat. 'She didn't time it too well,' he said. 'Another couple of minutes and I'd never have known. But I agree with Tom, she's a damn sight better driver than you'll ever be.'

'The sort of thing that could happen to anybody,' said Sarah, when Robina explained exactly what had happened as they went into the house together. 'I've done it more than once,' and Robina looked at her anxiously.

'You have? Then it's about time someone else was driving you or you were taking more care.'

'I know,' Sarah agreed cheerfully on both points. 'So you'll have to drive, won't you? Was Leo giving you a lesson?' She dimpled, and Robina said,

'We were talking about the furniture that was saved from the fire. Chris is seeing to it, but Leo said if there was anything he could do.'

'Are you selling?'

'I suppose so.'

'Then let Leo handle it,' said Sarah. 'He'd get better prices than Chris would.'

'I'm sure he would.' Robina shrugged the matter away. She could never tell Sarah how deeply she distrusted her brother, although one day Sarah would guess, because you couldn't hide hostility like this for ever.

She had the shakes. They had gone into the drawing room and as Robina sat down she looked at her hands and they were shaking. 'I feel awful,' she muttered.

'You look it.' Sarah dashed to a cabinet, pouring a small brandy. 'Here, drink this. You've got delayed shock, you'll be all right in a minute.'

'Of course I will.' But the glass rattled against her teeth. It was because she had come so close to causing a bad accident and because she had had to drive back with the pirate. She drank the brandy and closed her eyes and thought, I've got him under my skin; because her body was reacting now as it had wanted to react when he had shut himself in the little cabin of the car with her, screaming out in panic.

CHAPTER FOUR

In a few minutes Robina could smile and say, 'I'm all right now.' She had stopped shaking and the panic had eased. She started to babble, 'Until I did that stupid thing I was having a lovely time driving your car. We went all round the town and it was super. Tom was terrific. He spoke up for me when——' she gulped, the name 'Leo' always stuck in her throat, 'when your brother arrived on the scene. Tom said I'd been doing all right till then and it wasn't the sort of thing that would happen again.'

'Good old Tommy.' Sarah was still watching Robina closely, then she grinned. 'You know, I really thought you'd run into Leo's car.'

Robina grinned. 'Bad enough him getting a grandstand view. Trust me to come shooting out just then!'

'It is his home stretch,' Sarah pointed out. 'It's not that much of a coincidence. Although I don't know, it could always be fate.'

'What could?'

'Maybe you and Leo are meant to come up against each other.' Sarah's voice took on the thrilling quality of a melodrama queen, and she gestured ceilingwards. 'Perhaps it's all destiny. Written in the stars.'

She was fooling, but the joke didn't amuse Robina. No one had influenced her life more than Leo Morgan. Even when she never saw him his shadow had fallen across her every day, and now she was living in his house his physical presence frazzled her nerves. She thought grimly, I'd rather come up against a gorilla; and her smile was the merest twitch before she changed the subject. 'I'm still not happy about all those clothes. What's he going to say about them?'

'I've unpacked them.' Sarah started impulsively for the door. 'Come and see.'

Unpacked they seemed to fill the room. They were spread out on the bed, hanging from the wardrobe doors, and Robina bit her lip and shook her head. Sarah took down an afternoon dress, admired it at arm's length and said, 'Wear that for dinner tonight and then he can see what a good buy it was.'

'Who can?' Robina croaked, although she knew what Sarah was going to say.

'Leo, of course. He's in tonight. If you're stopping at home you'll have dinner together, won't you?'

The idea of a tête-à-tête turned Robina's stomach, and she protested, 'Not tonight, I'm just not up to chatting over a dinner table. Tonight I'll have a sandwich or a bowl of soup, anything, in my room, if I may.'

Sarah's smooth forehead furrowed. 'But it seems silly, both of you eating on your own.'

'I need to be on my own.' Robina couldn't tell Sarah that her brother at the table would make it almost impossible for her to get any food down. 'Seeing the Castle, the way it is, it's shaken me. I want to be on my own.'

'Sorry,' Sarah said after a moment. 'I think I understand. I mean, I can imagine how you must be feeling. I'll tell Leo we're both going out, then you won't be disturbed.'

'Thank you,' said Robina fervently. She supposed there would be times when she might find herself all alone with Leo Morgan—rarely, but sometimes, and she would have to consider whether the job was worth the risk. It was a job in a million, but that was a shattering prospect.

The dress for Friday night seemed to be Sarah's favourite. She told Robina how well it suited her and made her try it on again, and Robina thought how crazy it was that she should be here, in Morgan's house being treated like one of the family. She hoped Uncle Randolph wouldn't have considered it a kind of treachery, although the way it had happened had seemed almost preordained. 'Fate,' Sarah had just joked, and if it was written in the stars that was bad news up there for Leo Morgan.

Sarah's own dress for tonight's jaunt was smooth glittering gold, with a ruched front, several slim gilt chains and golden sandals. She reeled off the names of half a dozen folk she was going with. Some Robina knew, although she had not been part of the social round for years. These were the ones with money, the families that had not fallen on hard times.

She said, 'You'll be a knock-out. Pity Carlos can't see you.'

Sarah was brushing her pale gold hair and shrugging her shoulders in time to the music of a cassette, but when Robina said that she went very still, sitting in front of one of the dressing table mirrors. Her voice changed. Up till then it had been gay and giggling, but suddenly she sounded almost sad. 'We'll have fun,' she said. 'It will be a good evening, they're a good crowd, but I shall be missing him all the time.'

She meant that, Robina realised. This might not peter out as her brother hoped, as the others had. If there was trouble ahead it might worry Leo, but right now Robina was thinking of Sarah and feeling distinctly apprehensive for her.

Later from her bedroom window she watched Sarah leave, bright and flashing, getting into another luxury car from which voices and laughter rose; and then she settled down to answer some of the letters of condolence.

Perhaps they didn't expect answers, but she was confined to her room as she was supposed to have left with Sarah. She ate the cold meat and salad they had brought up earlier from the kitchen, and started with school friends, who had seen newspaper reports of the fire. Several had been holiday visitors to the Castle in the early days. Most of them said they would love to see Robina again, inviting her to their own homes, and who knows, the time might come when she would be glad to go visiting.

She wrote much the same few lines over and over, thanking them for writing, agreeing that her uncle had been a fine man and she would miss him dreadfully. Nobody would ever know how much, but she didn't say that, and she thought she was managing well as the pile of single sheets and addressed envelopes grew.

It wasn't until a stab of pain shot through her eyes that she realised what a strain she was finding it, and then she got up and went to the window and opened it and let the cool air blow on her flushed face.

She had heard the phone ring several times in the hour or so that had passed since Sarah went out. Phones seemed to be constantly ringing in this house, far oftener than they had in the Castle. In the last six months Uncle Randolph had had hardly any calls at all, but there must be people lining up to get in touch with the Morgans.

It was ringing again now as Robina leaned out of the window filling her lungs with air. She didn't hear the tap on the door, but Mrs Palmer probably did knock before she walked in—she was very particular about things like that. When Robina turned Mrs Palmer was advancing on her and announcing,

'Phone for you, miss, it's your brother.'

'Oh, thank you.' A call from Chris was always welcome.

'I noticed you didn't go with Sarah after all,' added Mrs Palmer, falling into step beside Robina.

'No, I decided not to.'

There was an extension phone in Sarah's room, but she went instinctively to the hall telephone. It was the one she had used before and it was off the hook, Mrs Palmer had taken the call there. 'Chris?' she said.

'Hi, baby. Are you all right?'

'I'm fine. Honestly.'

'Treating you right, are they?'

She laughed a little at that. 'Couldn't be kinder. Sarah's a sweetie. She's a wonderful girl.'

'So are you,' said Chris firmly. 'She's lucky you're staying. Now I've been in touch with Jarvis and Jephson'—a firm of local auctioneers—'and they'll be writing to you about doing an audit. You'll have to get everything valued for probate.'

The black cavern that was the main hall of the Castle flashed into Robina's mind and she shied away from it. She didn't want to talk about that strange still place, nor the smoke-stained, charred remains that had been piled into the outhouses. She said quickly, 'That's all right, then. Now, how are you? What are you doing?'

He was working, and next month work should bring him within fifty miles of her. Was there any chance of her meeting him? 'I should think so.' She was almost sure. 'I'd have to ask Sarah, of course, but she might like to come too, then I could drive both of us. She has a super sports car.'

She would have gone on to tell him how she had nearly smashed it this afternoon, sweeping out of the Castle drive, but the door of the study opened and Leo Morgan stood there. Robina was standing with her back to the wall, half sitting on the table edge, and their eyes met, his with raised eyebrow query, because Sarah had told him Robina would be out and now he had found her here.

'Sounds just the job,' said Chris. 'Keep your spirits up. I'll ring again soon, and anything you need, you know where to get hold of me.'

They exchanged goodbyes and the phone went dead, and

Leo Morgan said, 'Good evening. You changed your mind, then?' That was fairly obvious.

'There were some letters I decided I should be answering,' she said.

'Will you join me in a drink?' He was walking towards the drawing room, and if she had had any choice of course she wouldn't have joined him, but he added, 'I'd like to have a talk with you,' so it was an order, not an invitation.

Her first thought was, All those blessed clothes, I knew we were buying too much. It was going to be very humiliating being told off by the pirate for extravagance. She would have to make it clear that she was not a grabber, she didn't want the wretched things. But it would be putting all the blame on Sarah and she could hardly do that.

'No, thank you,' she declined his offer of a drink, and he said,

'I wish you would.'

Robina gave a small shrug. 'A small vodka and tonic, then, if I'm going to need a drink. If it's something unpleasant we're going to talk about.'

He poured for her, and a whisky for himself, and she sat down in one of the armchairs and he sat opposite, then he said 'What were you expecting that was unpleasant?'

Anything that you have to say to me, she thought. Sitting here with you is one of the most unpleasant situations I I could find myself in. The glass he had given her was heavy, with the slight roughness in the centre of the base that meant it was genuinely old. She ran a forefinger round and round the base and said, 'My driving this afternoon, or the clothes bill from this morning. I don't have any excuse about the bad driving, but I'm sure the clothes can go back?'

'Why should they?' He sounded surprised at the suggestion, so that wasn't what the talking was going to be about.

'So many,' she explained.

'You have to replace what you lost in the fire. It seemed a reasonable enough list to me.' Sarah must have told him what they had come back with, and of course he and Sarah lived in another style from the life Robina had known. She remembered her old wardrobe back in her old bedroom and she almost said that the models upstairs here were very different clothes. But she hesitated; he must have known the Jeffersons were feeling the pinch, but there was no need to emphasise their poverty, and before she could say anything he said, 'I wanted to talk to you about Sarah. I thought you were with her tonight.'

'No.' He could see that. He could see she was here. 'But she is with friends.' Did he expect her to stay close to Sarah day and night, perpetually on guard? His expression was dubious, and she said bluntly, 'She's a grown woman. You can't keep her in an ivory tower. You're her brother, not her keeper.'

It was rather like baiting a tiger. She was only talking sense, but she felt a little thrill of excitement wondering if she could make him lose his temper and raise his voice. She didn't. Leo half grinned at her and admitted, 'I've always felt more like her father than her brother, and there are times when she needs a keeper. Most of the men she chooses see money when they look at her.'

Robina hadn't expected him to confide in her; it took her aback and she blurted, 'But Sarah doesn't have any money, does she?'

'No.'

'You mean they see your money. And I'm sure you're wrong, because she's quite beautiful. Men would still fall for her if she was as poor as——' she was going to say, 'as poor as me', but she changed it to, 'a church mouse.'

Leo said, 'In theory she is. In fact of course she's all the family I have. I want a man for her who isn't looking for an heiress. Not like the last time.' His voice was still quiet. He was a big man, you could imagine him as a pirate, ranting and roaring, striding up and down on deck, the skull and crossbones flying overhead, that sort of nonsense. But suddenly Robina doubted if he ever needed to raise his voice to scare anyone out of their wits. When the lines deepened in his face, and his mouth became a cruel thin line, she could believe that if Sarah's husband had not died in the car crash her brother would have broken him.

Her mouth was dry and she said huskily, 'I'm sure it won't be the same again. She must have——'

'Learnt her lesson?' He finished the sentence as she paused. 'I doubt it. That seems to be the type she goes for, and the last time nearly killed her. She lost the child she was expecting. She nearly went out of her mind.'

Robina hadn't heard about the lost baby before, she didn't think that had got into the papers. Leo went on, 'I was abroad a great deal that year. I knew things weren't going too well, but I'd been against the marriage and I decided to stay off the scene, give them a chance to settle their differences. I expected her to get in touch with me if it got too bad.'

He sounded as though he considered himself partly responsible for Sarah's unhappiness, and Robina was deeply sorry for Sarah, but she could also feel for Leo in his anger and pain when he went to fetch his sister, after her husband's death, and learned what a hell the marriage had been.

The last thing she wanted was to start seeing anything from Leo Morgan's point of view, but she had to say, 'I'm sorry.'

'You know her track record?' They were neither of them drinking. They had put their untouched glasses aside and they sat looking at each other.

'I read the papers. They're not serious affairs, are they?'

Sarah always seemed to get her name linked with light-weight men, but the accounts of her escapades were always tongue-in-cheek paragraphs. Nothing that seemed serious.

'That letter this morning,' said Leo abruptly, 'did she tell you who it was from?' She didn't answer, but he knew from her face, and he said, 'He's a harmless enough lad, but she couldn't take that kind of life.'

Robina agreed, and yet Sarah had told her that she was missing Carlos all the time. Robina was for Sarah, and didn't want to side with Leo in any way, so she tried to detach herself from the problem. 'Really this isn't any of my business. Why are you telling me all this?'

'Because Sarah admires you. To listen to her you're a paragon of all the virtues.'

Her mouth fell open. 'Me? You're joking!'

Sarah had only known her a matter of days, and in that time nothing had been quite normal. She was glad that Sarah liked her, but there was no reason why Sarah should admire her.

'But you are fond of her?' asked Leo.

'Of course.'

'Then keep an eye on her for me, will you? When she talks to you try to get her to see a little sense.'

He made her feel a hundred years old. Was she supposed to advise Sarah not to fall in love with men who weren't rich? Sarah would probably laugh in her face and tell her to shut up. She said, 'I'm sorry about her rotten marriage, but you can't guarantee that the rest of her life will be plain sailing. And the men she chooses—well, couldn't you be wrong?'

'I can read men,' he said drily. 'Not women quite so easily, but men, yes. I can smell out the ones who are for themselves and nobody else, and those are the kind that Sarah finds.'

If he was such a good judge of character how was it that

he saw no value in Uncle Randolph——? And her tone
was tart. 'Are you some kind of mind-reader?'

'Of course,' he said with a surprisingly attractive smile.
Even while she was disliking him bitterly she noticed the
change that flash of white teeth, and the crinkle at the
corner of the eyes made. 'That's why I'm so revoltingly
rich.'

Robina hadn't expected him to joke about his wealth. She
would have thought that was a deadly serious subject. She
knew that he had started with his father's business and was
suddenly curious enough to ask, 'But weren't you always
rich?'

'Far from it.'

'Oh.' She shook her head and Leo asked,

'What does that mean?'

'I can't imagine you without everything going for you.'

'But you didn't know me at seventeen.'

That was beyond her too; no matter how hard she stared
there was no seeing behind the strong, experienced, intelligent face, and the broad powerful bulk of the man's body,
to the boy he must have been. 'Why seventeen?' she asked.

'I was seventeen when my father and my stepmother—
Sarah's mother—were killed in an air crash. They were
on a package holiday flight, the first holiday they'd had in
years.' Now he owned aeroplanes. He flew first class with
V.I.P. treatment. He must have forgotten what an economy
seat looked like. 'We had a factory about the size of this
room.' He sounded as though he had looked around more
than once and remembered that. 'Making period firebaskets
and very little money. Sarah was just four, and they started
talking about putting her into an orphanage, and that was
when I decided to become a tycoon.'

'So you did it all for Sarah?'

He grinned. 'I think I'd have done it anyway. Work and
power and money, I like them all.' You had to, of course, to

get where he'd got. You had to be pretty single-minded in your pursuit of the gilt-edged good life. 'But I started earlier than I might have done, to keep a home going and pay someone to look after Sarah.'

In those far-off days everything had been lovely for Robina, although she was an orphan too. The Castle was beautiful, and Uncle Randolph had seemed like the wisest man in the world, while Leo Morgan was fighting his way to this house and all his other houses. To their factory and all his other factories.

She said quietly, 'Well, I promise I'll do my best to keep Sarah happy.'

'Thank you.' His piercing eyes were looking straight into her eyes and she sat transfixed. 'But put like that it sounds a very one-sided arrangement. I hope you'll be happy here too.'

There was an obstacle to her ever being carefree and happy in this house: the man who was talking to her now like an old friend, telling her things she was sure that he rarely discussed. She wished she liked him and could accept the friendship he was offering her. But he was the pirate who had plundered her birthright, the man who had made Uncle Randolph weep and broken his heart and spirit.

She said, 'Thank you,' and stood up. 'May I go now, please? I still have my letters to finish.'

'And they must be answered tonight?'

She hadn't tasted her drink, and when Leo got up too she was scared he was going to cross to her, and touch her. He wanted her to stay down here so that they could go on talking, and she was anxious to escape. She couldn't bear him to touch her.

'Yes,' she said, 'they must. Now I've started I want to finish them. It isn't easy. They all say the same thing and I'm doing more or less the same answer, but that doesn't make it any easier.' She was walking towards the door, but she had to look at him because she was talking to him, and it was a wonder she didn't bump into anything.

'Of course,' he said, his deep steady voice contrasting with the jerkiness of her own words. He didn't move away from his chair, but as she went out of the room he said, 'Goodnight, Bina,' and she bit hard on her lip, answering, 'Goodnight.'

Sarah had asked if she might use that old pet name, but she hadn't, she had gone on with 'Robina'. And Chris had only used it after Uncle Randolph's death. It would be incongruous if Leo Morgan should end up as the one who called her by the name from her childhood, and how could she stop him, except by making a scene? It wasn't worth that, but she would resent it every time.

She didn't finish her letters. Instead she ran herself a hot bath and after that went to bed, reading for a while before falling asleep. Sarah coming home woke her. They were still shrieking and laughing in the car. Robina heard Sarah calling goodnight and promising to ring somebody on Monday, and was glad she had stayed here herself. She couldn't have stood hours of those voices, let alone the din of a nightclub. Although she hadn't had a very relaxing time here; Leo Morgan had made her sweat.

When she had got back to her room there had been little cold beads of perspiration on her forehead, and she had felt as worn out as though she had just finished a bout of hard physical work.

She curled up now, moving sleepily, hearing the car with Sarah's friends driving away. These other friends who would be coming to the dinner party on Friday, this girl Imogen who was Leo Morgan's 'sleeping partner'; would she be staying the night? Robina wondered. What would she be like? What would *he* be like as a lover? Oh lord, what a thought! What a ridiculous, revolting thing to start wondering about! The light bedding felt weighty as she struggled to get head and shoulders above the sheet, gasping for air, turning her head as though to escape something bearing down on her.

Any thought of Leo Morgan was stifling—he invaded her living space and now her sleeping space. Metaphorically speaking, of course, but it still seemed a liberty. Robina sat up and pummelled the pillow hard and found it none too easy to fall asleep again.

She didn't come downstairs next morning until Leo's car had left, this time with Tommy at the wheel. She watched through her bedroom window, then she went into the breakfast room, where the table was set for two and there was no sign yet of Sarah. By the newspapers was a letter for Robina addressed to the Castle. Her mail was being delivered here now. It was from a man who had been in the army with Randolph Jefferson in the war and hadn't seen him for twenty years. It was good to know how other men respected him, although Robina wished the man had written while Uncle Randolph was alive.

Mrs Palmer came in with coffee and asked, 'Not bad news, I hope?' catching her sighing over an account of how her uncle had saved this man's life.

'I've had all my bad news,' said Robina, and Mrs Palmer nodded sympathetically.

'Another one of them? You put them on one side, miss. They'll be a comfort to you later. It's too soon to be reading them yet.'

'I will.' Robina put it back in its envelope. 'And I wish you'd call me Robina.'

'All right.' There was a piece of paper torn from a notebook, a list, on the coffee tray, and Mrs Palmer said, 'Would you ask Sarah to have a look at it? It's the menu for Friday night.'

'I used to do the cooking for my uncle. Does Sarah choose the menus?'

'She runs the house, doesn't she?' Then Mrs Palmer smiled. 'But she's never chosen a menu yet, nor changed one, and I've been doing the cooking for a very long time. Between you and me she's not much use in a kitchen.' She said that with such affection that Robina asked,

'Are you the one who looked after her when she was a baby?'

'I am that.' Mrs Palmer's face glowed. 'Oh, she was a lovely baby. We lived next door, my Jack and me, and it was a bit different in those days, I can tell you, but you know he hasn't changed.'

'Jack hasn't?'

'No.' Mrs Palmer chuckled. 'Jack's changed. He's a first-class gardener now, he could write books on it. And I've cooked for some of the highest in the land. Oh, we've changed a lot, Jack and me. No. I'm talking about the master.'

She sounded as proud as a mother. The Palmers had hitched their wagon to a star when Mrs Palmer went next door to look after a four-year-old girl while a seventeen-year-old boy when into a tiny factory to make their fortune. If Leo Morgan hadn't changed he must have been an extraordinary boy, and of course he had. But the determination and the ruthlessness would be there at the start. He had grown in power until he ruled an empire, and although the Palmers had had a wonderful time travelling his road to success there must have been hundreds he had trampled on the way.

Like me, thought Robina. Like us. And her fingers closed over the letter from the man who had described Uncle Randolph as one of the finest gentlemen it had ever been his privilege to meet.

'One of the kindest men alive,' said Mrs Palmer, but she was talking about Leo and smiling at Robina. 'You'll be staying on, I hear.'

'Sarah's asked me to be her companion for a while.'

'Well, you'll be all right here,' said Mrs Palmer comfortingly, and Robina wondered if she could be thinking that perhaps the fire wasn't such a tragedy after all, because life must have been hard and lonely for Robina in Cliffe Castle and now she was living in luxury.

'I was very happy—we both were,' said Robina quietly, and the older woman put a hand on her shoulder in instinctive sympathy.

'I'm sure you were, my dear. Perhaps you should have a look at that.' She nodded towards the menu list. 'Tell me what you think about it, as you know about cooking.'

'Thank you, I'd love to.' Once Robina had expected to be organising dinner parties for guests to the Castle. It was a long time since there had been any lavish hospitality there, but she was genuinely interested in cooking and she looked with bright eyes at Mrs Palmer's menu.

The main dish—duck en daube—she knew, and they discussed the length of time the duck should be marinated in the wine and brandy, how much garlic and what herbs should be added for the simmering.

Lemon soufflé with Cointreau was a favourite with one of the ladies who were coming on Friday, Mrs Palmer informed her. The master rarely took the sweet course, and that didn't surprise Robina; but she noted that although Mrs Palmer still called Sarah 'Sarah', somewhere along the way Leo had become 'the master'. So much for there having been no change, and she wondered how old he was —twenty? twenty-five?—when he ceased to be 'Leo'.

She said, 'I suppose I couldn't do some cooking, could I?' She knew that cooks could be possessive about their kitchens. 'There's a summer lemon cake I used to make. Perhaps it could come on with the sweet course.'

'Of course it could,' said Mrs Palmer heartily. 'You come along to the kitchens any time and I'll show you

around.' She viewed Robina approvingly, deciding she was
a sensible girl and the sort of friend young Sarah needed.

Sarah laughed when Robina told her. 'It's always been
a nonsense Mrs P. bringing the menus along to me. I mean,
I know they're all right, she's a fabulous cook.'

'You're not, I suppose?' said Robina.

'Beans on toast,' said Sarah airily. 'Actually I'm pretty
cunning with toast.'

She was spreading toast with honey. She bit into it with
her small white teeth, pretty as pearls, and Robina said, 'I
came down to answer the phone last night and your brother
asked me in for a chat. About you.' Sarah wrinkled her
nose. 'He's worried about Carlos,' said Robina. 'He wants
me to ask you to cool it.'

'So you've asked me,' said Sarah.

There wasn't much more she could do, but anyone could
see there was little hope for a long-term relationship between Sarah Morgan and her young Spanish fisherman. A
short-term, yes, a brief and passionate love affair, but if
bad times came Sarah did not seem mature enough to
weather them.

'Don't worry,' said Sarah. 'This one isn't like the others.
He makes me laugh more than anyone else. He's crazy,
but he's clever.'

'He'll need to be clever,' muttered Robina. 'I should
think your brother's rather prejudiced against crazy men,
especially for you.'

Sarah gave a small nod of agreement. 'Leo does prefer
sensible folk. His women are usually sensible.'

'All of them?' asked Robina, thinking that any girl who
got involved with Leo Morgan would have to be right out
of her senses, and that made Sarah laugh again.

'Oh, there haven't been that many—work comes first,
you know, and only one at a time, but they all seem to be
the same type.'

'That's what he said about you,' said Robina, and wished she hadn't, seeing Sarah's face whiten.

'This time it's different.' Sarah's mouth set in a stubborn line. 'Because he's on my mind all the while. I can't stop thinking about him, and that's got to mean he's special, hasn't it?'

'I had a case like that myself once,' said Robina wryly. 'There was a man who got under my skin like nettle rash. Very special he was. One on his own, I hope. But that didn't mean I was in love with him, because I couldn't stand the sight of him.'

Sarah thought she was joking. She asked, 'Anyone I know?' and Robina said, 'No,' which was true. Sarah's beloved brother and the pirate were two different men. If Robina had described Leo Morgan as she saw him, and felt about him, Sarah Morgan would not have recognised one single detail . . .

At six o'clock on Friday night Sarah and Robina were visiting a recently married couple of Sarah's friends. It was an attractive flat, but it was about twenty miles away from the white house and the guests for the dinner party would be arriving around half seven, and Robina was getting worried.

She liked Sarah's friends, she would have been happy enough to spend the evening here, but there could be trouble with Leo Morgan if Sarah failed to turn up to act as hostess tonight. Sarah seemed fascinated with the apartment and openly envious of the newlyweds. 'You are lucky,' she said. 'It's super. Your own little home. Oh, all right,' she sighed when Robina reminded her how time was passing, 'I suppose we'll have to go.'

She sat silently looking out of the car window for most of the journey back, and when they reached the house she said, 'If we go up the side stairs we should get to our rooms without bumping into Imogen.'

Imogen Faulkner, Leo's girl-friend, was here for the weekend, expected during the afternoon, and although Sarah hadn't said much about her Robina had noticed that they seemed to be keeping out of Imogen's way. Robina hadn't asked any questions. Nor did she now as she followed Sarah upstairs.

'I'll come along to your room when I've changed,' said Sarah. 'Then we can go down together.'

Robina got out of her day clothes, and the grime of the day, and put on her evening make-up and the elegant grey dress. She brushed her hair until auburn lights gleamed in the dark waves, and as she sat waiting for Sarah the girl in the mirror looked almost like a stranger, poised and cool, an ice maiden with no fire in her. 'Well,' she said when Sarah walked in, 'will I do?'

'You'll do,' said Sarah. She had the expression she had worn at the beauty parlour, after Robina had gone through the treatment, smug and triumphant. 'Now we'll go and say hello to Imogen,' she said.

Leo Morgan and Imogen Faulkner were alone in the drawing room. He stood up as the two girls walked in, dark-suited, impeccably tailored, and the young woman who had been seated beside him on the pale green sofa smiled brilliantly. She wore a black dress, with one smooth naked shoulder that caught the light. 'Sarah!' she gave a little trill of welcome. 'How lovely to see you, and——'

She didn't seem quite so delighted to see Robina. 'Robina Jefferson, Imogen Faulkner,' said Sarah, and Imogen extended a languid hand so that Robina had to cross the room to take it. The moment Robina touched her she withdrew her fingers.

She must have heard about Cliffe Castle, but obviously no one had told her that Robina was here, and when Sarah announced, 'Robina's living with us, she's my companion,' all trace of the smile vanished and Imogen stared as though this was some strange specimen before her. 'Your *companion*? I thought only old ladies had living-in companions. How extraordinary! And what kind of qualifications does a companion need?'

'Whatever they are,' said Leo, 'Robina has them.'

'Has she now?' Imogen cried in simulated surprise. 'And whose little friend did you say she was?'

Robina held down a rising surge of indignation, and Leo asked what they would drink and where they had been all afternoon. Sarah named the friends and described the flat, and Imogen sat pretending to smile and obviously seething.

It was absurd, but she was jealous of Robina, and if she had been less aggressive Robina would have found some way to reassure her that her own position in this household was as platonic as Mrs Palmer's towards Leo. But as it was, as the evening progressed she grew less and less inclined to put Imogen Faulkner's mind at rest.

It should have been a very pleasant dinner party. Robina knew Roy and Celia Weske, the estate agent and his wife; and the other two men, Jack Grossmith, a Public Relations man from the factory, and Bernard North, the lawyer, were both very likeable. The conversation was entertaining. Leo Morgan was an hilariously funny raconteur; she would never have suspected what a keen sense of the ridiculous he had. He brought the others out too, so that the talk sparkled. Robina didn't say much, but she enjoyed listening had would have enjoyed it more if Imogen hadn't constantly contrived to make her feel an intruder.

Most of the time the snubs were subtle and could have passed as thoughtlessness, probably no one noticed but Robina, but after she had taken several glasses of wine Imogen became openly sarcastic.

The food was delicious, of course, and Sarah told them that Robina had made the summer lemon cake, with its intriguing combination of flavours, and while everyone was murmuring appreciatively Imogen drawled, 'Oh, you cook too? Oh, you're going to be a treasure around the house—upstairs and downstairs.' There was a second's silence, then Robina said, 'I hope so,' and Imogen asked,

'Were you trained for anything? I mean, you can hardly have expected to be offered a job as companion to dear Sarah. Did you ever have a job, a profession, a trade? Anything?'

'Not really,' said Robina. 'I expected to be lady of the manor, only we went broke. After that I was cook-cleaner-gardener.'

'Until the family pile burned down?'

'Yes.'

'I do hope,' said Imogen sweetly, 'you were well insured.'

'I'm sure you do,' said Leo, and that was that, because he began to talk about boats.

The guests left around midnight and Sarah and Robina said goodnight to Leo and Imogen in the hall and went upstairs to their rooms. Sarah was chattering about a coffee morning tomorrow and Robina was half listening when, at the door of her room, Sarah exclaimed, 'Hell, I've left my handbag downstairs!'

'Do you want it?'

'Yes, I do.'

'I'll fetch it,' Robina offered, and grinned. 'After all, I'm being paid to fetch and carry.'

'Thanks,' Sarah smiled too. It's under the chair I was sitting on in the drawing room.'

They were still down there in the hall. When she rounded the corner of the gallery Robina could see Leo and Imogen below, and Imogen was laughing and her laughter sounded odd.

Something checked Robina. This did not seem the time to be marching downstairs, and as she drew back she heard

Imogen say, 'Now I've heard everything. *I'm* to mind what I'm saying because *she* mustn't be hurt?'

'She's been hurt enough.' That was Leo's deep voice. 'It's only a couple of weeks since her home burned down and her uncle dropped dead, and if you lack the sensitivity to appreciate that just keep your mouth shut. You were baiting her continually tonight, and I will not have it.'

'Staying on, is she?' drawled Imogen.

'Yes.'

'Well, perhaps there isn't room for both of us.' Imogen's shrillness was almost a shriek. 'Perhaps you'd like me to leave?'

'Please yourself.' Then footsteps crossed the hall and a door closed. Robina guessed that was Leo; if Imogen had walked away she would probably have slammed the door, and she beat a hasty retreat herself, down the thickly carpeted corridor towards the bedrooms.

She didn't want Leo Morgan's pity, but there was a queer sort of confused comfort in knowing that, while she was here and whether she wanted it or not, she was getting his protection ...

'That was quick,' commented Sarah, as Robina came into her bedroom, and Robina shrugged, showing empty hands.

'Sorry, but you'll have to fetch your own handbag. I nearly walked into a row down there. They were still in the hall.'

'Leo and Imogen?' Sarah knew the answer to that. She didn't wait for Robina to speak before she asked, 'What was the row about?' and immediately started to laugh. 'About you, was it?'

She had kicked off her shoes and was sitting on a stool in front of the dressing table, looking mischievous, and Robina demanded, 'Are you trying to cause trouble be-

tween them? Is that what I'm doing here? You're not over-
fond of Imogen, are you?'

'No, oh *no*!' Sarah's shock at the accusation seemed
genuine. 'I've got nothing against Imogen, it's got nothing
to do with her. I want you to stay because I like having
you here, I like you very much. I'm sorry she was a bitch
tonight, and I suppose it isn't all that funny that Leo got
mad at her. He did get mad at her, I suppose?'

'Yes,' said Robina.

'And she deserved it. I could have told her a thing or
two myself, but she isn't around here much, we can always
keep out of her way.' Sarah was pleading now, worried that
Robina might be offended, and Robina smiled,

'All right, but I'm not going downstairs again tonight.'

'Oh, I'll fetch my handbag.' Sarah came across the carpet in stockinged feet. 'I carry him around with me, you
know, and sleep with him under my pillow. It's only a
photograph, but it's better than nothing.'

Bernard, the lawyer at tonight's party, had seemed a
nice man, but he would never make Sarah's eyes shine like
this. 'Sweet dreams,' said Robina.

'Most nights they are,' said Sarah. She smiled and bit her
lip, then padded off down the corridor, her white dress and
loose fair hair making her look very young.

Sometimes the dreams were sweet, but other nights she
must be frightened and lonely. There wasn't much joy in
this house tonight, thought Robina. Mrs Palmer had prepared the room for Imogen, next to Leo's room, but she
had been threatening to leave just now, and he had been
doing nothing to stop her.

She wouldn't leave, of course. She had probably followed
him, opening that door he had closed, and after a few more
words had been tossed around they would start to smile at
each other. Because they were lovers and it was late.

Robina went to her own empty bedroom. There was nothing unusual about that, her room was always empty, but tonight she heard herself sighing as she stripped off her make-up and got into bed. She was tired, she was going to sleep. Breathe deep, breathe slow, she told herself, make your mind a blank. But while she tossed and turned and tried to find a cool and easy place she couldn't stop wondering what Leo was doing to Imogen.

CHAPTER FIVE

THE table in the breakfast room was laid for two when Robina came down next morning. That could mean that Leo and Imogen had eaten already, or that they were breakfasting in bed. There was no sign of anyone, although it was nearly half past nine. Robina had slept heavily when she finally fell asleep, and she sat down now and picked up the only letter on the table, which was addressed to her and looked businesslike.

The heading was Jarvis & Jarratt, Auctioneers and Valuers, and someone with an illegible signature was telling her that her brother, Mr Christopher Jefferson, had been in touch with them over the proposed valuation of the remaining contents of Cliffe Castle. Would she kindly write or telephone with instructions when it would be convenient for an audit to take place?

The sooner the better, she thought, wondering if anyone would answer Jarvis & Jarratt's phone on a Saturday morning. As soon as she had had a cup of coffee she would dial their number and find out, and she was just getting up from her chair when the door swung open and Sarah came in, carrying a coffee pot and grinning from ear to ear.

'Hey, guess what?' said Sarah. She began to fill one of the cups. 'Imogen took off at first light.'

'What?'

'She did.' Sarah swung the pot over to the second cup. 'Drank three cups of black coffee in a stinking mood, and didn't even leave a note. Mrs P's just told me.'

'Does your brother know?' asked Robina.

91

'Yes.' Sarah helped herself to milk and sugar, and when Robina muttered, 'Oh dear,' she grinned again.

But it wasn't pleasant, causing friction. If Robina was staying on she determined to keep out of Imogen's way; she would always try to keep out of Leo's. She drank a little of the very hot coffee, and Sarah leaned across to the letter from the auctioneers and asked, 'What's this about?'

'Read it,' said Robina, which Sarah was doing anyway. 'I was just going to ring them. Should you think there'd be anyone in the office?'

A girl answered and Robina explained who she was, and what the letter she had received this morning had contained, and she was put through to a Terence Hawkins, which she supposed must have been the strange scrawl of a signature. He knew Chris personally, and he sounded anxious to be helpful. In fact they could start the audit today, this morning, if Miss Jefferson could be at the Castle in—say, half an hour's time.

She didn't want to go back, so she said, 'I think everything's in the outhouses. I suppose they're locked up, but I don't have any keys.'

He did he said, so why, she wondered, must she go over? 'About half an hour, then?' he repeated, and she said, 'All right,' steeling herself.

In the breakfast room Sarah was still reading the morning papers and Robina informed her, 'They're going to start making their lists in half an hour and they want me around.'

'They're quick off the mark,' said Sarah admiringly. 'You won't need the car, will you? I mean, you can go in the Mini?'

'Of course.' She could have walked it in half an hour, down the steps cut in this cliff and round the beach of the bay, and up the path to the lawns of Cliffe Castle, but she didn't want to climb that path alone. She didn't want to go to the Castle alone, and she asked, 'I suppose you couldn't come with me?'

Sarah looked crestfallen. 'Well, I did promise Sandie—her coffee morning, you know.' The coffee morning would be more fun. It would be gloomy for anyone over at the Castle, dirty and dismal, and as Sarah was saying, 'I mean, there's nothing I can actually *do* over there, is there?'

I should have liked someone with me, thought Robina. Someone who wasn't a stranger. But it seemed this was something she had to do alone, so she said quickly, 'That's all right, I shan't hang around. I'll just look in and see what's going on.'

'Then you could come on to the coffee morning,' said Sarah brightly. 'You know the address.'

The town was about five miles away, and Robina said, 'I'll probably do that,' and knew that she wouldn't because no matter how helpful Mr Hawkins was, and how quickly she got away, the next hour or two would leave her in no state for chattering over coffee cups in a room full of strangers ...

It had to be done, and she had to stay calm, but she felt sick turning into the drive of the Castle at the wheel of her little car. She went very slowly, coming to a halt more than once, looking at the windows with the flaring pattern of scorch marks around them. All glass had gone. In some of the windows it had been coloured, there had been motifs and designs, but now there was just emptiness.

The stone carved faces, high up, were supposed to be portraits of the men who had built the Castle. When they were children Robina and Christopher had named them all, and the one she was staring up at now was Samuel. He was blackened with smoke, and she said, 'Sorry, Sammy, there's nothing I can do about it.'

Demolition was the likely course, and most of the furniture and paintings that had been salvaged would have to be sold. Robina drove round to the front, on to the lawns that she now realised were churned up and scarred from the night of the fire. Another car was parked alongside the coach house and stable block, and she got out of her Mini and walked across.

The doors were open, and furniture was stacked where several carriages had once stood. So long as Robina remembered it had been a garage, but now it looked like a junk shop, and at first glance she spotted the leather wing-backed chair from the small drawing room, in which Uncle Randolph had passed the last evening of his life.

A man came between the furniture. He was youngish, balding and bespectacled. 'Miss Jefferson?' he said. 'I'm Terence Hawkins.' They shook hands and there was a woman with him, carrying a clipboard, saying, 'Good morning.'

Nobody smiled. This was an aftermath of tragedy and Robina knew they would be more at ease, and able to get on with the job better without her. But first there was talk, about probate, and what she was hoping to keep and what was likely to be auctioned, as they walked around.

The coach house seemed very big and barny, not a good storage place. Draughts came in and she was shivering, but of course it was safer than leaving the stuff in the house and Chris must have organised the clearance in the days when she couldn't even bear to look over here.

She wished that Chris was with her now; she felt dreadful, although she was trying to sound normal. 'I expected to see everything scorched and black,' as she spoke she realised this was only a fraction of what had been the contents of the Castle, and she went on, 'Is the rest still in there?'

'Some's in the stables, but this is the repairable marketable stuff.' Terence Hawkins added wryly, 'The rest's in pretty bad shape.'

'I'll go and see,' she decided.

In the stables were the casualties. Some of the pieces in here were unrecognisable, and she should not have lingered. But they had the fascination of horror for her, and she walked past the piles of broken and burned debris, picking out here and there something that retained its old shape.

She found part of a Louis Quinze chest that used to stand in her bedroom, reminding her what might have happened if her uncle had not come to warn her of the fire. Their headlong flight had saved her life, if not his, and from looking at that the next stage was to look at the house.

She came out of the stables and walked along the gravel path to the front door of the Castle. The boards nailed across the opening with their scarlet warning, DANGER, KEEP OUT, left room for her to squeeze underneath, and the woman who was helping with the audit, and standing in the doorway of the coach house, said, 'She's gone inside there, I hope she knows what she's doing.'

It was dark, in what had been the entrance hall. Although you could see straight up to the sky everything down here was matt black. The great oak staircase with its carved handrail was charred and partially burned away, and beams and debris from the upper storeys made a hideous obstacle course.

Robina picked her way, slowly and carefully. The pointed archways in the stone walls surrounded blackened swinging doors, and she looked into each room on the ground floor. Some were gutted; some had almost escaped. Most were empty, and she walked with her memories until she reached what had been the kitchens.

Everything in here seemed twisted and distorted, and black. There was so much blackness that the red tin tray with its pattern of white hearts, that she had carried in here with their supper mugs, seemed like a flash of dazzling colour. It was scorched and blistered, the hearts weren't white any more, but the bright cherry-red paint still showed.

She dug a tissue out of her skirt pocket and started to rub it very gently, and when she heard someone calling, 'Bina, where are you?' for a moment she was transported back to her childhood. 'In here, in the kitchens.' As she spoke she knew that was Leo Morgan's voice and she bit her lip too late, and turned frantically for some way of escaping him.

The door leading outside was blocked, the way she had come would take her towards him. She went through the first opening up winding stone steps, dropping the tray with a clatter. This was one of the little towers, up to the roof, part of the Gothic image. It would have been a smoking death-trap on the night of the fire; steps and walls were still tacky with a tar-like substance, but the steps were sound.

Robina heard Leo shout, 'Come down, it isn't safe!' and she yelled, 'Go away!' then heard him coming and went higher. Two doors that should have opened on to corridors opened into space. She kept close to the wall and went up, step by step. She was convinced Leo would stop. It was a narrow winding staircase and he was a big man, heavy. He might stand and bellow after her, but he wouldn't follow her right up to the roof.

When she reached the roof she clapped a hand over her mouth to stop herself screaming. There wasn't much of the central area left. She wouldn't have dared peer down into that great pit, waves of nausea were threatening her now, but when she heard him still coming she stepped out of the turret along the ledge of stone battlements, edging the wall.

Only a few steps. It seemed solid enough, but there might be cracks. She held on to the parapet and glared through a tangle of dark hair at the man who appeared in the turret aperture, and had the nerve to shout, 'For God's sake, girl, what do you think you're doing?'

'Looking,' she yelled back. 'Just looking.'

'Well, now you've seen it.' He was coming out on to the stonework and she shrieked, 'Don't you do that! It might not stand your weight.'

'I'm aware of that, but I'm not leaving you up here.'

He thought she was crazy, up here for the view. When all she was doing was running from him, and now she couldn't run any further, and she had to come down. 'All right,' she said. 'I'm coming.'

Leo waited for her and then stood aside and made her go down first, close enough behind to grab her if she fell, or —and this might be how he was thinking—took a suicide leap on the way. On the other hand, if he slipped they could both end in a heap at the bottom. 'Watch the steps,' she warned, 'they're slippy.'

'I noticed on the way up,' he told her.

By the time she reached the kitchens her surge of near-hysteria had subsided and she was controlled enough to ask him coldly, 'What brings you here?'

'You do, of course.' He looked at the palms of his hands, grubby as hers from using the smoky walls as support, and wiped them on his jacket. That would need cleaning. 'Sarah told me where you'd gone. You shouldn't have come here on your own.' He sounded as though it was her fault she was alone, so Sarah couldn't have mentioned that Robina had asked her to come over. It was strange that Leo had realised what an ordeal it would be for Robina while Sarah hadn't. But then he had seen her belting out of the drive last time.

She said, 'I was only walking around the ground floor. I wasn't planning to throw myself from the battlements or anything like that. I just ran when I heard you calling me.'

If he hadn't come she would have shed a few tears, maybe, and then walked out again. 'Why,' he asked, and she couldn't think of any other answer. She said simply, 'I didn't want to see you here because I think you killed him.'

'I did *what*?' He sounded unsure he had heard aright.

'My uncle.' She turned her head, looking around. 'This caused his second heart attack, but you caused his first. The slight one he had just after you took over the firm.' As she put it into words it was a monstrous accusation, although she had thought it a hundred times, but Leo's voice was quiet, almost gentle.

'You think that wouldn't have happened if I hadn't taken over? You think it would have been easier for him to be made bankrupt?'

Robina looked down at the tin tray, lying near her feet, and the events that had brought her to this, mourning her dead in the ruins of her home, seemed complex and inexorable. Leo was no more to blame than the lightning strike, or the order books that hadn't filled, or the strain on Uncle Randolph of running to save her that night. She admitted at last, to herself as well as to him, 'No, of course it wouldn't have been easier. And this would have finished him. He wouldn't have wanted to go on living when he saw this.'

'Come on.' He didn't touch her, but his hand was near her arm, guiding her, and she stooped to pick up the tray.

'We had our last supper together on this,' she told him. 'I bought it a few months ago because it was cheap and cheerful.'

'Leave it.' Leo took it from her and put it on the charred surface that had been part of a Welsh dresser. 'Hold on to the good memories.'

There were plenty of good memories. They crowded into her mind, but with them came loneliness, and she said, 'He was always so good to me. He saved my life that night because I didn't know a fire had started. I shouldn't have got out if he hadn't come for me.' She started to shake and Leo put his arms around her, and somehow he wasn't the enemy any more. She could feel his strength flowing into her. Her face was pressed against his soft cotton shirt, her cheek prickled by the coarser stuff of his jacket. She breathed the clean man smell and it was good after the stale tainted air.

He held her without speaking until she was strong enough to stand alone, but he still kept an arm around her until they were out of the kitchens and through the entrance hall. There was only one plank now across the doorway, he must have torn the other down to get in; and Terence Hawkins and the woman with the clipboard stood in the middle of the lawns, both looking rather strained.

'Whatever were you doing up there?' the woman shrilled, and Robina realised that she had been spotted on the roof, with her hair streaming in the wind. Probably they had been standing here since they had told Leo where she was and he followed her into the Castle. She said,

'Just looking around. I think I've seen all I want to see. I think I'll leave you now.'

She sounded steady, but she wasn't sure she should be driving, and she was about to ask if she might travel in Leo's car when he suggested, 'Shall we walk back, along the beach? The cars can be collected later.' After the briefest hesitation Robina said, 'I'd like that,' and they walked together, away from the Castle towards the trees and the shrubbery and the path down the cliffs.

They passed a clump of trees where Uncle Randolph had stood with tears on his cheeks after that meeting with Leo Morgan, because there was no place for him in the new set-up. But if the family firm had been on the edge of bankruptcy the changes that swept through it had been necessary. She would always miss her uncle, and never love him less than she did now, but the bitterness was slipping away. She couldn't go on hating a man who had welcomed her into his home, and come looking for her this morning because he knew that she would be feeling sick and sad and lonely.

The scent of the sea was in her lungs, the lovely salt taste refreshing and renewing her as she stepped out a pace or two ahead of Leo. Nothing was said, but she could hear him light-footed behind her, and it was strange what a feeling of security that gave her.

She knew the narrow winding path down the cliffside well. She had often walked this way to the beach, usually alone and always with worries on her mind. Her uncle worried her, their poverty and the bills coming in. How long she could keep the Castle going. Now the Castle had gone and nothing could hurt Uncle Randolph again, and the man walking with her was an ally, powerful and kind.

She had learned that about Leo grudgingly at first, that he was kind. This morning her reaction had been to run from him, although he was ready to risk his own neck getting her down from the roof. Her mind had accepted the logic that he was no ogre, personally responsible for Uncle Randolph's failing health, but a vestige of her prejudice might have lingered if he had not put his arms around her.

When he had held her close, and she felt the hard strength of him, the pain had melted away. It had been an instinctive primeval thing. Her mind went along with it, but the pressure of his arms around her body, and the warmth of his breath on her cheek, spoke a wordless language, as though he reached inside her and touched her heart . . .

It was not a private beach in this cove, but it was a few miles from the nearest holiday resort. Even on a warm summer's day like this there was only a young family—mother, father, and two brown naked children—building a sand castle, an older couple walking with a dog, and a man sitting on a rock reading a newspaper, a straw trilby hat tilted over his eyes. Nobody was taking any notice of anyone else, and Robina stopped to take off her shoe and tip out a few small sharp pieces of gravel.

The sand was firm and clean and it would feel nicer walking barefoot, so she didn't replace her shoe. She shook off the other, and her tights, rolled her tights into a ball and put them in her pocket. Leo had walked to the water's edge. That was his boat out there, and she could understand him liking to look at it, because it was a handsome sight. If it had belonged to her she wouldn't have been able to keep her eyes off it.

When she reached him she said, 'She is a beauty.'

Leo smiled at her. 'Are you fond of boating?'

She was a good swimmer, but it was a long time since she had been invited to join the yachting parties. 'Uncle Randolph wasn't much of a sailor,' she said. 'We used to mess about in other people's boats when we were down here on school holidays, but we never had one of our own. Chris was more for cars.'

The sun was bright. Robina put up a hand, shadowing her face, and she didn't realise that her eyes were wistful as she watched the white boat moving gently in the currents.

'I'm going out,' said Leo. 'Will you come?'

'Oh, please! When?'

'Now.'

'Oh *yes*!'

'I've got to go up to the house first,' she told him.

She went so fast that he laughed, keeping pace with her. 'If I'd known there was a chance of going out in the boat I'd have come back by car,' she said, and she ran most of the way along the beach, hurrying up the cliff steps and arriving in the gardens of the white house with a jabbing stitch in her side. 'I'll be right back,' she gasped, leaving

Leo in the hall. 'I've just got to change and write a note for Sarah.'

She wasn't dressed for sailing. She was in a grey silk shirt and a beautifully cut grey skirt, part of the wardrobe Sarah had provided. Both were marked from her scramble up the tower, but they were elegant and expensive and she mustn't risk getting them into an even worse state.

The trouble was she didn't have any cheap clothes. She could have used a pair of her old jeans and an old shirt right now, but all she could come up with was a dress that could be hand-washed. She washed herself, and as the grime flowed away she realised that she was light-headed with excitement. Going for a sail wasn't such a big deal, surely, but it was a beautiful boat and a beautiful day, and she had come through the trauma of seeing the burned-out Castle and she felt as though a weight had fallen from her shoulders.

She was downstairs telling Mrs Palmer where she was going when Leo came out of the study. 'Ready?' he asked.

'Yes.'

'Any message,' said Mrs Palmer, 'if Miss Faulkner should decide to come back?'

'She won't, said Leo. 'Not this weekend.'

It seemed a long time since Robina had overheard that argument between Leo and Imogen, and as she was the subject of it she was partly responsible for Imogen Faulkner clearing off this morning. She was glad that Leo didn't seem too concerned. Imogen would obviously have been sailing with him today, and that was something else Robina was glad about. That Imogen wasn't and she was ...

Robina felt at home from the moment she stepped on to the deck of the *Achilles*. Tommy, who had piloted the little dinghy with its chugging engine that brought them out, looked very different in ragged slacks and blue T-shirt from the neatly uniformed chauffeur; and a man with grizzled hair and whiskers, every inch the old sailor, welcomed them aboard.

He seemed surprised to see Robina, he must have been expecting Imogen, but he shook her heartily by the hand when Leo introduced him as Niall. He lived on the boat, she found, the *Achilles* was his home and his way of life.

Everything was as shiny bright as though it had been painted or polished that morning, and Robina heard herself murmuring, 'Oh, it's beautiful, oh, isn't it beautiful?' while the men grinned in agreement.

She sat on a side seat in the prow as the fifty h.p. engine took them out of the bay, watching the outline of the Castle against the sky. It still hurt to realise it was only a shell, but she couldn't look away until Leo came and sat beside her. 'Don't look back,' he said, then she turned and the clear sky and the open sea spread out in front of her like a new life of infinite horizons.

She said, 'You're right, it's a better view. May I explore?'

Leo let her go alone and she liked that, because it meant she could roam as she pleased, peering into anything that intrigued her. There was a fair breeze blowing and the sails were going up, but there was a guardrail running the entire length of the boat, the deck was non-slip and she was barefoot and sure-footed.

She went down into the teak-lined main cabin and the little fitted galley. After the nightmare of the Castle everything was so fresh, so gleaming clean, that it seemed to her there was all you would need here to sail around the world. A cooker and sink, seats and a table, a loo-and-wash compartment, bunks.

In the main cabin the long seats down either side would be used as beds, one would convert into a double if you pulled out the board underneath. This would be where

Leo and Imogen slept, she supposed. There were other bunks in other places, but this must be the master-bedroom, as it were.

She supposed they did spend nights on the boat. The *Achilles* wasn't a day-trip craft, it was an oceangoer. Robina thought, I wish I was sailing right away; and she sat down, swinging her feet up, clasping her hands behind her head, lying flat.

Spray spattered the porthole like rain, except that the sun was shining through it, and the sound of the engine had ceased, so they must be under sail. This was very comfortable, a super bed; she could sleep on this any time.

She didn't hear anyone coming until Leo chuckled and then she shot upright. 'I'm making myself at home,' she blurted. 'Trying everything out.'

'You do that.' He went through into the galley, and she sat watching him. It should have been ridiculous, seeing Leo Morgan fiddling about with pots and pans, but he was deft and quick, and she was sure he could handle any job aboard like an expert. 'How long have you been a seafaring man?' she asked.

He looked across at her and smiled, 'A boat was the first thing I bought, with the first money that wasn't spoken for.'

Robina could understand how a little floating home would be an ideal escape from the stresses and strains on land and promised herself, 'If I have any money left maybe that's what I'll do. Not like this, of course, but something I can sail away in.'

'Do you want to sail away?' he called.

'Who doesn't?'

'Would you sail back?'

She laughed, 'Why should I? What's waiting for me, except a peck of trouble?' That sounded like a joke, but there was truth in it, and Leo didn't laugh.

'Your friends would miss you,' he said.

'Yes.' Chris would miss her, and a few other people. Sarah for one, maybe. But no one would sail after her to bring her back. She leaned over the half-section dividing the galley from the cabin and asked, 'Can't I take over in here? I'm handy in a kitchen.'

'Not today. Today you're on holiday. Next time you can take your share of the chores.'

Robina was glad to hear there would be other times, and today *was* a holiday. The three men treated her as though she was queen for the day, and she suspected that Tommy and Niall also knew that she had spent a dark hour in the Castle this morning.

They put themselves out to see that she enjoyed herself, showing her how everything worked. She tried her hand at steering, by the wooden tiller, and Niall said, 'There's a clever child,' when she got the knack of it. She looked enviously at the throttle and gear lever of the engine and wondered if she might get a chance some time to try them.

There was an easy camaraderie between the three men. Leo, who was 'sir' to Tommy on shore, was 'skipper' here. Tommy, Niall and the skipper. Not 'Leo', although there was no rank pulled and no orders given. He was dressed as casually as they, in striped shirt open to the waist, slacks and bare feet, but he still had the power aura. He was the natural skipper, Captain Morgan.

Robina remembered that when they were drinking from cans of beer, sitting together in the sun on the deck, and said, 'Captain Morgan shouldn't be drinking canned beer. It should surely be rum.' She had meant to say that very lightly, but there was a slight huskiness in her voice and Leo looked at her with keen dark eyes.

'We used to call you the pirate,' she explained. 'It was our nickname for you. My——' she hesitated, and gulped, 'My uncle's and mine.' She smiled brilliantly and Leo's voice was bantering.

'With Morgan for a surname I've been called a pirate more than once. He ended as a reformed character, you know—Sir Henry Morgan, Governor of Jamaica.'

'Reformed?' Robina's delicate brows arched and he winked, leering like a villain in a melodrama.

'Or getting the best of both worlds, the wily old devil.' That made her laugh, and she knew that if she ever used the nickname again it would have no resentment in it, it would be a joke. Leo understood that any mention of her uncle was painful to her and he was coaxing her into the giggles; he was a really nice man and she was very glad that he was her friend.

They came back into sight of land as the day ended and skirted the coastline, the men pointing out landmarks to her so that she was kept in a continual state of astonished recognition. 'Oh *yes*! Good heavens, so it is!'

She wondered whether they would have turned back if she hadn't been aboard or if the original plan was to spend the whole weekend afloat, anchoring off France, perhaps. If Imogen had stayed would she have been sleeping tonight with Leo in the bunk that could turn into a big bed?

He was taking the *Achilles* in by engine as they approached their own bay, and Robina stood beside him. The Castle and the white house were both visible, but one was dark and empty while lights were going on in the windows of the other. The white house was her home now, and the lights seemed to be shining a welcome.

She said, 'It was a grim start to the day, but the rest has been wonderful.'

'I'm glad.' His height seemed immense when she was right beside him, he dwarfed her, and she said,

'You've all been very kind. I've felt as though it was my birthday and I was about ten years old.' She laughed, 'It's a long time since anyone called me a clever child.'

'You're no child,' Leo said quietly, 'you are very much a

woman,' and she was suddenly as aware of her body—the rise and fall of her breasts, the warm soft suppleness— as though she stood naked. Her bones seemed to be liquefying. She didn't need to say, 'And you're very much a man,' when he was so overpoweringly male.

The look between them lasted no longer than a few seconds before he turned his head, but while their gaze locked Robina felt as though she was being dragged towards him and holding back took all her strength.

When he looked away she realised how desperately she had wanted him to touch her. If he had she would have gone as close to him as she could, in any way she could, and she wouldn't have cared who saw her. She had never before experienced that flare of heat and hunger, that left her whole body burning although the air was cool now that night was falling, and she began to babble, 'It's been a lovely day, I've had a lovely time, I'm sorry Imogen——'

She stopped there. To say she was sorry that Imogen had cut short her stay would have been a thumping lie, and Leo said, 'No need to be sorry,' and smiled at her until she smiled back.

She knew that some day soon, or some night, he would reach for her and she would respond passionately, because the sexual magnetism between them was so strong. She attracted him, and for the first time in her life she was near a man who could make her ache just by looking at her.

She had been wrong in hating him, that had been blind bigotry, but this had to be almost entirely physical, because she didn't know him that well. Really she hardly knew him at all, and perhaps she should be making plans for leaving his home. She was at risk while she stayed, but she had run from Leo for the first and last time this morning, and at the moment she could think of nothing beyond the time when she would go into his arms and let him love her.

CHAPTER SIX

ROBINA had not been mistaken about the physical rapport between herself and Leo. She was so conscious of him during the days that followed the sailing trip that she believed she could have walked straight to him in pitch darkness, and when he came into a room he looked for her and when he saw her he always smiled.

Sarah noticed what there was to notice: the smiles, the friendly talk, Leo's help with Robina's problems. The salvaged contents of the Castle were now safely stored in one of his warehouses, his solicitors were helping with the probate of the will, and by his instructions interior debris was being cleared and plans for restoration were being drawn up. Chris said he was delighted to hand over the responsibility and Leo had delegated to experts, and Robina was free of immediate material worries for the first time since she had left school.

Sarah noticed all that, and seemed pleased that Robina and Leo were getting along so well. She made little jokes about it, and Robina laughed at them and agreed, 'Of course he's super, he's a marvellous man.' But this wasn't a friendship based on kindness and gratitude, and getting to know each other. Well, it was on the surface, but Sarah never guessed how Robina lay awake at nights, racked by yearning, waiting for a knock on her door.

The relationship between Robina and Leo Morgan was potentially explosive. The tap on the door would come, or the look or the word, and it would be like the lightning striking again.

She daren't think about afterwards, nor how long an

affair might last. Imogen Faulkner hadn't been back; perhaps Leo was seeing her, but if he was it was not general knowledge and Sarah said she didn't think so. A letter arrived two weeks after the dinner party—and the sailing trip—while Leo was away at one of his other factories, and Sarah declared the writing on the envelope was Imogen's.

'Oh?' said Robina, carefully cutting her toast into very thin strips. 'Do you suppose that's on again?'

She wasn't jealous. Her instincts told her that right now she was the woman Leo Morgan wanted, and he had no time for playing the field. 'Never more than one at a time,' Sarah had told her, and Sarah said now, 'I've heard she's saying he's got to come and fetch her but she'll have a long wait. He's never run after a woman in his life and he never will. If they go away they can stay away.'

Leo had brought Sarah home more than once, but then she was his sister and all the family he had. 'He's fetched me back,' she said, echoing Robina's thoughts, 'but that's not the same thing at all, is it? And the next time I go it will be for keeps.'

'You're going somewhere?'

Sarah smiled her secret smile. 'Oh, I'll give you plenty of warning. Maybe you could come with me.'

'Where to?'

'You mean, who to?'

Sarah was still in touch with her dark-haired lover. She had gone out alone several times, and when she came back Robina knew she had either phoned him or received a call from him. She never said so directly, but it was obvious enough, and she nearly always talked about him for a while afterwards. He sounded a heart-throb, with all the local girls after him, but faithful now to Sarah. Robina asked no questions, she knew the answers wouldn't be reassuring and a discussion could turn into an argument.

Sarah didn't want anybody's advice, but this was the first she had said about leaving home again. Going to Carlos probably meant setting up home with him, even marrying again.

'Have you decided you can manage without your allowance, then?' Robina asked, and Sarah shrugged. 'You couldn't get a job out there very easily.' Robina didn't add that earning a living anywhere wouldn't be easy for Sarah, who muttered,

'Leo might change his mind. Anyhow, we might have enough to get by before long.'

'Are you saving?'

'Who, me?' Sarah chortled, and it was a silly question when she was so extravagant.

'I shouldn't have thought a fisherman would have been making very much——' Robina began, and Sarah wrinkled her nose,

'Oh, that's the family business, he's always hated that. It bores him, he's an *artist*.' She sounded as though Robina should know that, and perhaps the gossip writers had mentioned it. Sarah hadn't to Robina's recollection, but she had definitely said that they would need her allowance and a struggling artist could be very hard up, so Robina doubted if Leo would be impressed.

'What sort of pictures?' she asked.

'Out of this world,' said Sarah rapturously. 'They really make you see things differently. He has this fantastic perception.'

'Do you have any of them?' Sarah shook her head. 'Do they sell?'

'Oh yes,' said Sarah. 'And one day he'll be famous—you see.'

'Are you going to marry him?' Robina asked bluntly, and for a few seconds Sarah didn't reply. She had propped Leo's letter up against the milk jug while she inspected

Imogen's handwriting, and she looked at it again, head on one side. Then she straightened up and met Robina's gaze with unblinking eyes and unsmiling face.

'Very likely,' she said. 'But that's our secret, isn't it? You wouldn't give me away to Leo, would you?'

Leo never mentioned Carlos these days. He seemed reassured that Sarah was content with her friends and her way of life, and although it wasn't a very useful life it was an enjoyable one. Robina enjoyed herself. She went most places with Sarah, shopping, visiting friends, driving into the countryside to eat at recommended places. They went swimming in the bay and out on the boat. Leo and Tommy weren't with them this time, but Niall had another man, a nephew of his, to help him, and there were young friends of Sarah's who sunbathed on the decks.

Robina earned her salary. She acted as hostess with Sarah when Leo brought home business contacts, or friends were entertained. Mrs Palmer and Jack had always managed very well, but Robina's interest and help in the house and the garden pleased them. 'A born lady,' Mrs Palmer described her. 'Real quality she is, and a very fair little cook too.'

'Honestly,' said Sarah, 'I don't know what we did without you.'

Robina was putting a couple of darts in the bustline of a dress for Sarah, while Sarah leafed through a fashion magazine. Leo had just come into the room and picked up a newspaper. The girls were chatting, but when Sarah said she didn't know how they'd managed without Robina he looked at her over his *Times*.

'It seems to me,' said Sarah, 'that you have all the domestic talents,' and Robina supposed she must look like a study in domesticity sitting there stitching away, but that didn't stop her feeling a fool.

'Don't you believe it,' she said, 'there are plenty of

domestic talents I'm right novice at,' and met Leo's amused eyes and looked hastily down at her sewing.

'Such as?' Sarah challenged, and Robina did an exaggerated shrug.

'Too many to start rattling off. Come and try this on, will you, I'm not too sure about it.'

One of the 'domestic talents' in which she had had very little practice for a girl of twenty-two was lovemaking, because she had never met a man she really wanted before. It couldn't be skill, so it would have to be instinct on her part, but Leo had the experience and she felt that the moment he kissed her, like tinder waiting the touch of flame, she would be consumed.

She wanted nobody else. She wrote back to the man who had once said he loved her, and whose letter of condolence had suggested a meeting, and said she was working for a living now and very, very busy. She looked around at the men who were Sarah's friends—not Sarah's lovers, just members of her social set—and knew that most of them would have been delighted to start something going. There were compliments and propositions, but none of them quickened her pulses. Some of the men were eligible and unattached, but they never shut Leo out of her mind.

One of the nicest outings, from Robina's point of view, was the day they spent with Chris and his TV team. Sarah was all for it when Robina told her about the phone call, and the two girls set off early morning to drive fifty-odd miles. The filming was round a new theatre, converted from an old barn by an enthusiastic bunch of young unemployed actors. They were calling themselves the Barnstormers, and planned to put on Victorian plays, mostly melodramas, to summer audiences.

The building and converting had been going on for some time, and progress had been followed by the TV team in fleeting visits. Now the next two weeks would see com-

pletion and the team was down to record the final touches
to the theatre, rehearsals of a forgotten gem called *I
Couldn't Help It*, and, as a finale, opening night.

Robina hadn't been along before, she hadn't been leaving Uncle Randolph much during the last six months, and
when she drew up in front of the brightly painted building
she turned to Sarah and burst out laughing. It looked so
gay and cheery, and although any theatrical venture had
to be a risk these days you felt that somebody round here
was having a lot of fun.

'What's the joke?' Sarah asked, and Robina had to admit, 'I don't know, but doesn't it look smashing?'

She parked the car, alongside several others, and by then
someone who knew her—Jimmy Allman, TV sound
recordist, a bearded soft-spoken man—was hurrying over
to them.

Robina had met the team on her visits to Chris, they were
old friends to her, and Jimmy had always made it clear that
he considered her attractive. He was divorced and he'd
taken her out during her trips to London, and tried with
even more heat than Chris to persuade her to leave the
Castle and move into Chris's apartment. She had smiled
and stayed stubborn, the Castle and Uncle Randolph both
needed her, but now she was free and Jimmy had been
keeping an eye open for her arrival.

It was a full day. They watched the filming and the inter-
views, inspected the theatre with its Victorian decor of
dark red and gilt, and saw the company rehearsing. Sarah
swanned around, as pretty as any of the young actresses,
and Robina tried to get it across gently to Jimmy that although she was no longer tied down with responsibilities
she was still not available.

Everybody saw them off, the TV team were staying at
a local pub, and they promised to come back in two weeks'
time for the Big Opening Night. Chris kissed both girls,

and Jimmy kissed Robina, and as they travelled along Sarah remarked, 'Jimmy fancies you, doesn't he?'

'So he says,' said Robina, 'but I don't really fancy him.'

'Nor me,' Sarah giggled. 'He reminds me of a great big motheaten teddy bear I used to have.'

That was a superficial judgment. James Ullman was intelligent and talented, and Robina liked him better than any of the other admiring men she had met with Sarah. Except Leo. And it wasn't that none of them compared with Leo, although in fact they didn't, it was because she felt as exclusively committed as though she wore a gold band on her wedding-ring finger. Of course she looked at other men, and talked with them and joked with them, but they could have been lumps of wood for all the sexual impression they were making on her ...

Sarah and Robina were in the audience for the Barnstormers' first night. It was a full house, seating capacity was only a hundred and fifty, but when the theatre was packed with a goodhumoured audience, booing and cheering in old-time fashion, a riotous time was had by all.

The Victorian playbill gimmick might catch on, or it might not, but at the buffet and punchbowl party afterwards well-wishers mixed with the cast, still in their crinolines and pantaloons, and congratulations were the order of the day.

The TV team were leaving at first light, and Robina and Sarah set off for home just after midnight. They turned on the car radio and played cassettes and were driving along under a starless sky, across a bleak stretch of road, through rugged countryside, when the car faltered and gurgled and came to a juddering halt.

'What happened?' Sarah had been silent for miles, apparently dozing, curled in the passenger seat, but this jerked her upright, and Robina bit her lip to stop herself saying, 'We've stopped,' because any fool could see that.

She said, 'I don't know. We're not out of petrol.' The lights were still on, so it wasn't that kind of power failure, but nothing at all happened when she turned the ignition key, and beside her Sarah was wailing.

'There's nothing out here. Not a light, not a house, nothing. Do you understand anything about engines?'

'Oil and water I can manage,' said Robina, 'but I can't see myself flashing a torch under this bonnet and trying my luck. Sorry.'

'We'll have to find a phone box or a house, and ring a garage or the A.A.' Sarah hunched down in her seat, pulling up the collar of her pale mink jacket, and Robina reckoned this was where she started earning her pay. Today's outing had been more for her benefit than Sarah's, she was the one who had wanted to see Chris. 'We'd better get it off the road,' she pointed out.

'How?'

'Shove it,' said Robina succinctly, and as Sarah stared, 'Come on, give me a hand, unless you'd rather take your chances of getting clouted while I'm hunting for that phone box.'

That moved Sarah, and although Robina did most of the pushing Sarah was the one who was gasping when they finally got four wheels on the grass verge. The car tilted slightly, but the ground was firm, and Sarah scrambled quickly back inside.

Outside was a cold night with a chilly wind and patches of fog, and Robina, wearing a silk dress and a velvet jacket, and high-heeled thin-soled shoes, could hardly have been worse equipped for setting off into the darkness.

It was bitter after the cosy heated car and as she got the torch out of the glove compartment Sarah asked dolefully, 'Do you want me to come too?'

She was clutching her fur coat around her, Robina felt she might have offered the loan of that but didn't feel like asking for it. Sarah looked waif-like and pathetic, her eyes wide, waiting to be told what to do, and Robina said, 'There's no sense both of us getting frozen,' although she couldn't resist adding, 'Shut the door, you're sitting in a draught,' as she stepped back on to the road.

She kept going for a mile. In that time one car passed her but ignored her flashing torch, and she couldn't blame them. This was heathland and it was late. She was a shadowy figure, they weren't taking any chances. But the mist seemed to be thickening, getting through to her bones, and she still couldn't see any lights.

The nearest town, she reckoned, was about five miles away; and then she put down her foot on an uneven patch of road surface, and the heel of her shoe folded neatly under and hung flapping. That settled it. She couldn't do five miles, especially in odd shoes. She was going back to the car.

The other heel proved remarkably strong. It wouldn't bend or break, and in the end she walked hoppity-fashion, which was tough on the calf muscles. She was glad to see the car, somewhere to sit down. The lights were off and as she tapped on the window Sarah raised a pale blonde head and a pale scared face. 'It's me,' said Robina.

'Oh, you poor darling!' Sarah opened the door. 'Is it raining out there?'

'It's the fog coming up.' Robina's hair stuck damply to her forehead and her teeth were chattering. 'And it's so cold.'

'Isn't there anyone with you?' Sarah peered out and Robina said,

'I didn't find a phone. I turned back.'

'Oh, you *didn't*!' Sarah gave a strangled cry and Robina breathed hard. Sarah had been warm in here while Robina was trudging through the cold, but Sarah, it seemed, was shocked that Robina hadn't staggered on till dawn.

'So what does it matter if we're stuck here all night?'

Robina demanded. 'At least it's warm and dry. It's absolutely foul out there. I've had all I can take of it, especially as I don't think there's a town for miles, and it's too dark to see houses that aren't slap on the road and I didn't seem to be passing anything but fields and hedges. But if you want to have a go don't let me stop you.'

After about five seconds Sarah said, 'Oh!' and Robina said, 'If we both stay with the car, and put all the lights on, then they can see we've broken down and it's a genuine S.O.S.'

'Of course.' Sarah switched on the headlights and the foglights and the interior light, and then settled back in her seat, and Robina was tempted to stay in the car and hope that a rescuer would draw up beside them. But she was so chilled she couldn't see much hope of ever getting warm again except in a hot bath, so she decided on a final effort and suggested, 'You wouldn't like to stand by the road for a few minutes and try to flag a car down?' Sarah's expression was horrified and Robina said, 'No, of course you wouldn't. Okay, go back to sleep.'

'Are you going to stand outside?'

'For five minutes. If there's no joy by then I give up.'

'Give me the torch,' said Sarah, sounding like a martyr.

Robina let her stand outside until there was a little warmth in her own freezing fingers and toes—the five minutes weren't quite up—then she got out of the car herself. Sarah was standing on the grass verge, looking down the long dark road into the eeriness of drifting fog. When she turned Robina gasped because the torchlight showed tears on her cheeks.

It wasn't the fog. Her eyes were swimming, and she blinked and sniffed, and Robina asked, 'Whatever's the matter?'

Sarah managed a watery smile. 'Oh, I am a fool, but suddenly everything seemed so—*lonely*. You know, everything so far away. As if I'd said goodbye for the last time, or something.'

It had been a pretty potent punchbowl and Sarah must have drunk much more than Robina. Robina was stone sober, and she said, 'You try to get to sleep,' then as she took the torch from Sarah's limp hand she saw the lights and screeched, 'There's something coming—oh, *surely* they'll stop!'

It was a long-distance lorry, and the two men aboard couldn't have been more helpful. They looked at the engine and diagnosed a faulty ignition. Something had become disconnected that they put back on, and wham! the car purred into life.

Robina was so grateful that she would have liked to accept their invitation to a cup of tea or coffee at the transport café, just outside the town up the road, but getting Sarah home took priority. So with heartfelt professions of thanks the girls drove away.

Sarah had dabbed her face dry with a tissue, and within a few minutes she was nestled deep into her fur coat, apparently sleeping soundly. It was then that the tiredness struck Robina. It had been a long day for her and a heelless shoe wasn't making the driving any easier now. She would have loved that cup of coffee, and she looked longingly at the lights of the all-night café when they passed it, but Sarah was sleeping and they probably wouldn't be home before morning as it was, without wasting any more time.

Fog made the rest of the journey seem long and tedious and a never-ending effort. The only way she could stay awake and alert was by not relaxing for a second, while Sarah slumbered beside her and the night sky lightened from black to dark pewter grey.

When they finally drew up at the Morgan home her eyes felt as though they had pepper in them and all of her ached. She slumped over the wheel, head on folded arms, and Sarah groaned, 'What an awful night!' and Robina's lips twitched in a wry grimace. She wouldn't have thought it had been all that awful for Sarah, who only seemed to wake when the car stopped.

Then the door beside her opened and she blinked her red eyes at Leo, who was bellowing in her ear, 'Where the hell have you two been?'

Perhaps he wasn't actually shouting, but his voice cracked like a whip, making her flinch, and Sarah got out of the car and walked round to him and said, 'We were at a theatre and we were late leaving because there was this party. Then the car broke down and we were stuck until two nice men came along and mended it for us.'

Robina stayed where she was, rubbing the back of her neck. Sarah was yawning, her tousled hair framing a peaked little face, and Leo told her, 'You'd better get to bed.' Then he turned to Robina. 'I suppose it never occurred to you that you might have phoned through here?'

'No, it did not,' she said. She was worn out and fed up. When they had set off, after lunch, they had told Mrs Palmer they would be back before midnight. It was morning now, and the night had been foggy, but Leo was carrying on as though it was Robina's fault that he hadn't known Sarah was safe.

If Tommy had been doing the chauffeuring no doubt it would have been part of his job to phone here and report the delay. But Robina hadn't thought, and why shouldn't Sarah do her own phoning home? It seemed it was part of Robina's job. At a time like this it was surprising how quickly she and Leo became employee and employer.

He was only concerned about Sarah. He had sounded very concerned telling her to get some rest, but now he was glaring at Robina, ordering her, 'In future tell somebody where you're going.'

'But of course,' she said. 'If you'll fix me up with a walkie-talkie I'll report every hour on the hour.'

'Don't be ridiculous!' He was still glaring at her and she would have liked to glare back, but her eyes were stinging so badly that she couldn't hold a stare for longer than three seconds before she had to blink.

Sarah plucked at her arm, 'Oh, come on,' and she got out of the car. She wanted to tell both of them what they could do with their job, but her head was woolly with fatigue, so that would have to wait. She stepped out, her walk ungainly in her ill-matched shoes, fuming that Sarah hadn't said a word in her defence. Leo had come on like the Victorian father again—and the Victorian employer—and Sarah hadn't even reminded him that there was no law against them coming home with the dawn. If he had minded his own business and gone to bed they'd have been back before breakfast.

When they reached the top of the stairs, with no signs of Leo behind them, she demanded, 'Why don't you stand up to him? Why do you let him treat you like a child?'

But a cherished child. He had just bullied Robina outrageously and her impression of him as a kind and considerate man had taken a big jolt. Kind when it suited him but callous when he was riled. Anyone could see how exhausted she was, but there had been no suggestion that she needed rest. He had just cracked the whip over her head.

'Because I don't want to get him mad,' said Sarah. 'Not now.'

They were at Sarah's bedroom door and having started yawning Robina was finding it hard to stop. She had to clench her jaw to ask, 'What's so special about now?'

Sarah looked up and down the empty corridor, then dropped her voice to a whisper, 'He's in England.'

'Who is?'

'Who do you think?'

Robina's bleary eyes opened wide, because Sarah had to be talking about Carlos. 'How long has he been here?' she gasped.

'Quite a while.'

'What are you going to do?'

'I could take your advice and stand up to Leo.'

'Why not?' Robina was too tired to care what might happen if Sarah confronted her tycoon brother with her hard-up lover.

'I'll sleep on it,' said Sarah, leaning forward again, her lips brushing Robina's cheek. 'You're such a comfort to me,' and Robina started yawning again.

She could have done with some comforting herself when she crawled wearily into bed, but she would not be listening for the tap on the door because Leo would not be coming, tonight nor any night.

He had never seriously considered her as a lover or he would have taken her days ago. He was not a man who waited. Robina was a useful employee, but he didn't want any closer involvement, either physical or emotional. And her infatuation for him was as immature as a schoolgirl crush. She would soon get over that, she wasn't going to moon over the bully who had glared at her tonight as though he wanted to yank her bodily out of the car and shake her . . .

She slept late, and when she woke she didn't hurry because she had earned a lie-in and she still expected to be downstairs before Sarah. Just outside her bedroom she met Mrs Palmer carrying a cup of tea. 'Nasty time you had last night, then?' said Mrs Palmer sympathetically. 'The fog was very bad here, we were very bothered about you. He made us go to bed, but I didn't get much rest until I heard the car.'

She sounded as though she had included Robina in her concern, which was nice of her and more than Leo had.

'The car broke down,' explained Robina, and Mrs Palmer nodded; she knew about that.

'Sarah said to let you sleep, but I thought you might like a cup of tea.'

'I would, thanks.' Robina took it from her, taking a sip as they walked down the corridor together, asking, 'Is Sarah up?'

'Up a long time ago.' Robina was surprised to hear that. 'And gone out,' Mrs Palmer continued. 'She left you a note.'

The note was on the breakfast table and Robina didn't open it immediately. She let it lie there, in its sealed envelope, while she finished drinking her tea, because what was inside could only be trouble and she was feeling jaundiced about the whole set-up.

Sarah had used her. She had been an unknowing cover-up for Sarah for goodness knows how long, and if Leo thought Robina had slipped up by not ringing last night, when the car broke down, he was going to go spare when he heard this.

Robina was supposed to be in Sarah's confidence, but she hadn't had a clue that Carlos wasn't still in Spain. Perhaps she hadn't wanted to know. She couldn't have babbled to Leo and she would have felt dreadfully uncomfortable keeping a secret like that from him.

She fingered the envelope, looking at 'Robina' in Sarah's large flowing script, and thought, No prizes for guessing where Sarah is. With Carlos. Although if anyone asks she'll expect me to lie, and say she's at the dentist or visiting somewhere. I've probably lied before, if he's been here for 'quite a while', but I was just repeating what I was told and I didn't know I was lying.

Maybe she would paper-clip Sarah's letter to her own resignation and leave both on Leo's desk. That should explain everything, and no prizes either for guessing which note would be pushed aside. Her resignation would simply save him the trouble of sacking her, but he was going to be furious at the way Sarah had fooled him; and Robina didn't think there was a hope in hell that he would go on paying her allowance so that she could finance Carlos while he painted his pictures.

She slit open the envelope, and Mrs Palmer came in with a tray as she took out the single sheet and read, 'I've decided to take your advice. Will phone you this evening, 6.30. *Please* say nothing about anything till then.'

'Will you be in today?' Mrs Palmer asked, arranging the contents of the tray on the table, and Robina murmured,

'Er—no, not until this evening.'

What advice had she given Sarah? Except, last night, telling her to stand up to Leo.

'Everything all right?' Mrs Palmer was noting Robina's worried expression, and Robina almost confided in her. She had helped to rear Sarah, perhaps she would understand about Carlos, but the emphasis of that underlined *please* seemed to leap out, and after a moment's hesitation Robina said, 'Everything's fine.'

It was so obvious there was something in the letter that she waited for Mrs Palmer to demand, 'What's Sarah got to say?' but with a final hard look at her Mrs Palmer went, and Robina poured another cup of tea with a shaking hand.

Sarah wasn't coming back tonight or she wouldn't need to phone. Standing up to Leo could mean telling him she was with Carlos. But if she wasn't planning to break her news face to face she would either have to speak to him on the phone or leave it to Robina.

When she first came here Robina had imagined herself doing that, and believed she would enjoy seeing Leo worried that Sarah was heading for heartbreak again, but now she wanted no part in it. The Morgans had employed her, and helped her, and she had tried to give back fair value, but they could deal with this development between themselves. She had done with being the middle-woman.

She couldn't face breakfast, she could only manage another half cup of tea, and then she went up to her room. She would wait for Sarah's call tonight, and tell Sarah that her job here was finished and she was leaving. There would be hardly any packing to do, nothing that wouldn't go into the boot of the Mini. Almost all her clothes had been paid for by Leo, and even if she was entitled to them she didn't want them. She had bought a few things herself with her salary and she could carry those down to the car this evening.

She would go to Chris and start life afresh from there. This new start hadn't lasted long, but perhaps the next would be a winner. There was nothing to keep her here. She was free of the Morgans, but she wasn't entirely free of the Castle. She had stopped worrying since Leo had taken it over, so to speak. The furniture was being auctioned next month, that would go ahead, that was all right. But the Castle itself, she didn't want that being left on her hands without a buyer.

Leo had been considering it for a conference and management training centre. Anyone buying would have to rebuild and nobody else had shown the slightest interest. Nothing had been signed, and they could be parting on bad terms, but when the costing figures cames in Robina couldn't see him letting personal matters affect his decision.

She put on a light coat, it was a warm day, and took a writing pad and envelopes out of a drawer. Then she went to the garages and got into the Mini. As she drove up the drive she saw Jack in the gardens. He waved to her and she waved back and thought, I shall miss helping you. I shall never see the gardens in autumn or winter or spring.

Her heart felt like a lump of lead in her chest and when she approached the turn for the Castle she almost kept going. The impulse to leave it all behind was strong. If I had that boat, she thought, they wouldn't see me for years; and pain stabbed her at the memory of the *Achilles* because that day she had believed she could never run from Leo again and tomorrow she would be putting as many miles as possible between herself and him.

She would wait for Sarah's call, then she would face Leo. If he was reasonable she would leave quietly in the morning. If he started ranting she would walk out there and then. She had never been Sarah's keeper and neither was he, and she would tell him that before she went. Just as she had told him at the beginning.

She would keep out of the house all day, so that no one could ask her questions about Sarah that she couldn't answer; and the obvious place to go first—as she was off to Chris tomorrow—was the Castle. She must look in at that before she left, and then she planned to go down on to the beach and write a few letters.

She had been over here several times while the demolition work was going on, and she had herself in complete control now. Everywhere the black horror of the fire was being cleansed away, and a new interior would be built if Leo went on with his project. If he didn't, and if no other buyer came forward, she was lumbered with a ruin.

The foreman, friendly, stockily built and freckled, greeted her with a grin. He was proud of the rate at which they were removing the charred woodwork and rubble and carting it away. 'Not bad, eh?' he remarked, as she stood in the empty doorway, looking into the vast shell that had been Robina's home and contained almost everything that was precious to her. She wondered if he expected her to say, 'Splendid, it never looked better,' and managed to sound impressed, telling him, 'You certainly aren't wasting any time.'

'Mr Morgan's orders,' said the foreman cheerfully. They

were on Mr Morgan's payroll and if he changed his mind about buying she wondered if he would send her a bill for all this. That made her smile wryly; of course he wouldn't, he knew what her financial position was, but she was wishing now that she had had something with his signature on, an agreement to buy and a price fixed.

'Leave it to Leo,' Sarah had said, and she had been ready to let him deal with everything. She had looked on him as a friend, she had looked on him as a lover. He had hardly touched her, but she had carried a hunger for him that had filled her days and her nights with longing. It had blinded her to her own interests and she hoped she wasn't going to regret having been so unbusinesslike. And she hoped that when she was away from him the longing would get less.

She sat on a rock, on the beach below the Castle, and wrote her letters to several friends, giving them Chris's address. She made the notes chatty and lively, as though she had been having a recuperative holiday here and was now ready to start afresh, and had decided that London offered the opportunities.

There were boats out in the bay, but not the *Achilles*, and when Robina had finished her letters she sat watching them. She wouldn't be here again for a long time. The last time Leo had been with her, and if she closed her eyes she could still feel his arms around her as he had held her in the burned-out kitchens of the Castle. 'Hold on to the good memories,' he had said, and she had many good memories of her stay in his house. She had led a pleasant life as Sarah's paid companion.

But the memory that would have mattered most she did not have, and she would always wonder—how would it have been with him? Perhaps it would always be the wrong face, the wrong body. It might be the right mind and spirit, because surely some day she must fall in love, but how awful if this frustrated physical passion for a man who did not

want her left her unable to give herself fully to anyone else.
She mustn't think like that. She could shackle herself with
inhibitions thinking like that, and she scrambled to her
feet.

She went into town, and ate a meal of ham salad and a
slice of cheesecake although she had no appetite, then
wandered around the shops until they began to close at
six o'clock. Then she drove back to the white house.

Sarah's call should be coming through any minute and
she went into the hall through a side door, hoping to slip
upstairs unnoticed. She would prefer to take it where no
one could see her and the best place was probably Sarah's
room. She could sit on the bed in there and grab the receiver at first ring. If anybody picked up another extension
that was just too bad. It wasn't going to be a long chat. All
Robina was going to say was goodbye and good luck.

She had her foot on the bottom step of the staircase when
the study door opened—it had probably been ajar, he
sounded as though he had been waiting for her—and Leo
said, 'Bina.'

'Don't Bina me,' she wanted to say, but the prospect of
taking Sarah's call with Leo watching closed her throat so
that she could only gasp.

'What's all this about?' He was holding a crumpled piece
of paper. Sarah's note? She had screwed that up and
dropped it into her bedroom litter basket. She should have
taken it out of the house with her, got rid of it outside, but
her mind had been screwed up too and she had never stopped to wonder if anyone might go rooting through her
wastepaper.

Leo turned back into the study and she followed him; he
put the piece of paper on the desk and it was Sarah's note.
Her voice shook with indignation. 'How dare you? What is
this, a police state?'

'You tell me what it is.' He was sitting down, in the big

swivel chair behind the desk. He indicated another chair, but Robina ignored the gesture. She didn't want a seat, she wanted to get out. The hooded lids turned his eyes into dark slits, but he was missing nothing, telling her in his slow deep voice, 'I come home and Mrs Palmer announces that Sarah went off with a suitcase this morning, leaving you a mysterious note. She went looking for the note. Not ethical but understandable.'

It was understandable that Mrs Palmer should worry about Sarah, but they couldn't protect her for ever. Robina said, 'Sarah is a big girl. Why don't you let her live her own life?'

'That was your advice, was it?' His eyes dropped to the note and she shrugged.

'In a way I suppose. I told her to stand up to you.'

'It's a man, of course?'

All Sarah's escapades included men, and a rackety crew they had been; she was a rotten judge of male character. But if she had gone to Carlos nobody could drag her away, and Robina faltered,

'I think she really cares for him, so why don't you give them a chance?'

Leo's smile was grim. 'Would I be right in thinking they want my money more than my blessing?' and she wished she could have assured him that this one wouldn't touch a penny, but all she could say was,

'He's an artist, he isn't rich.'

'Do I know him?'

'Yes, but——' But Sarah should be putting her case here not Robina. 'I don't know what to say,' she said. 'I don't know what to tell you. She should be phoning——'

He checked his watch. 'Two minutes late. Not much sense of time, our Sarah, we could have a long wait.'

Robina stared at the two phones on his desk, a business line and his home number, and willed the home phone to ring ... 'Ring, please—damn you, *ring* ...' because as soon as Sarah spoke she was going to hand over to Leo.

This was a family affair, and she would have said, 'You wait for it,' and walked out now, if her tongue hadn't been sticking to the roof of her mouth, and her legs had been steadier.

Then it rang, and Leo picked up the receiver, listened for a moment, then handed it to Robina without saying a word. She clutched it, gulping, as he went out of the room, across the hall into the drawing room, shutting the door behind him.

She could hear Sarah, 'Robina? Are you there? Hello? Hello?' and she licked her dry lips and croaked,

'Your brother saw your note, I've just been getting the third degree from him.'

'Is he there?'

'I'll get him. You talk to him.' She shouldn't have let him go, why had he gone? But Sarah's shriek, '*No*, I want to talk to *you*!' made her put the receiver reluctantly back to her ear.

'Well?'

'What did you tell Leo?' demanded Sarah.

'Not much.' Her legs felt like rubber and she walked round the desk and sat down in his chair, from which she could see straight across the hall to the closed door of the drawing room.

'I'm sorry I dashed off this morning, but I was so miserable yesterday,' Sarah was saying. 'All the way back in the car I kept thinking, I can't go on like this.'

Robina managed a wry smile. 'Now I would have said you were sleeping.'

'Oh *no*!' Sarah's denial had the ring of truth and it was possible that she had been suffering, not sleeping, although Robina couldn't imagine what had brought on the depression. 'They were so pretty, those girls.' What girls? The

Barnstormer actresses? 'And I thought, He's seeing girls like this all the time in his job and I should be with him.'

It was like listening to something in an alien language. Robina's mind was whirling and her head was aching. She asked wearily, 'What are you talking about?'

'Hello, love,' said a man.

'Chris? Is that *Chris*?'

'Of course it is.' What the dickens was Chris doing there? Did he know Carlos? Had they gone to him?

Then it was Sarah again. 'You knew, didn't you? You guessed.'

Guessed what? That Sarah had gone to Chris? That it was Chris, not Carlos? And she heard herself falter, 'But Laura——'

Chris now. 'Laura's still around, she's still got a room here, but we split up months ago.'

That was how Chris's affairs were, a lot like Sarah's. They had that in common, but it wasn't a reassuring link, and Robina asked jerkily, 'How long has it been you and Sarah?'

They must both have had an ear to the earpiece because Sarah answered, 'We met in a TV studio when they were trying me out for that commercial.'

'But that was before you went to Spain?' Robina was trying to get some order into this. It was just confusion to her so far, and Sarah giggled, and Robina could imagine her nose wrinkling and the dimples appearing in her smooth cheeks.

'Carlos didn't count,' Sarah gurgled, 'and it didn't hurt to make Chris a little bit jealous. He'd let me go without asking me to marry him. And it fooled the gossip writers, didn't it? And everybody.'

She sounded delighted with herself, but she had probably hurt Carlos and she had wasted Leo's time. 'Why bother?' Robina demanded. 'Why couldn't you just admit you were seeing each other?' and this time Chris answered, speaking very slowly as though he really wanted her to understand.

'We liked each other as soon as we met, but we needed time to decide if it was more than that, and Sarah does get more than her share of publicity. We felt we could do without our every move being reported in the press, so we kept things quiet.'

Robina said bitterly, 'Didn't you just?' and his reply was quick and defensive. 'Look, I knew how you and the old man felt about Leo. You weren't going to welcome Sarah with open arms, and I didn't think Leo would approve of a footloose self-employed cameraman making up to his sister.'

'Very Romeo and Juliet,' said Robina tartly. 'You don't have to worry about Uncle Randolph any more, but why should Leo have changed his mind?'

Chris said, 'He didn't know you then. He's got to believe there's something to be said for me when I've got such a gorgeous sister.'

'Don't talk such rubbish!' She wanted to bang down the receiver. She had the feeling of being crowded into a corner, manoeuvred into an entirely false position. 'What have I got to do with it?'

'You could have quite a lot,' said Chris, and Sarah's eager voice ran on, 'Will you talk to him? You get on so well with him. You're everything he admires in a woman.'

'Am I hell!' With every word they were making it clearer to her how obtuse she had been and how involved she was. 'What am I supposed to tell him?' she demanded. 'That you've moved in with my brother and give him the address to send your allowance?'

'Well, yes.' The irony escaped Sarah. 'Not as bluntly as that, but I don't have anything you see unless Leo forks out, and Chris is going to be famous one day but——'

'So you said, but I thought you were talking about

Carlos,' Robina broke in savagely, and Sarah gave a little incredulous squeal.

'Oh, you *didn't*! Not really you didn't! Chris said not to tell you outright, didn't you, darling? because he thought it would be better if you sort of came round to it. But you must have known I was always talking about Chris. Everything I told you was about him. And the photograph, I left that in my handbag all the time. You didn't ask to see it, but surely you took a peek.'

'I'm not in the habit of going through other girls' handbags,' said Robina stiffly, and wondered why she was bothering to say that, except as an excuse for missing every clue. It wasn't fair, I didn't cheat and you did. Like a child, outsmarted in some game.

Maybe there had been clues in their looks, in the way they spoke to each other. Sarah said there had been evidence galore and Robina was beginning to believe it. Right from Sarah's first description of her lover, 'dark curly hair and a touch of the devil', bringing Robina back here, talking about 'sisters'.

Sarah had gone to so much trouble to glamorise Robina and present her in a 'suitable' light to Leo because she was in this house as Chris's ambassador, and she resented it fiercely. She wanted to scream at them down the mouthpiece, but her voice shook, choking with hurt.

'You should have told me in words of one syllable instead of leaving me to use my wits, because I don't seem to have any. I'm thick. I'm so stupid that I believe what I'm told.'

'Love, don't take on like this.' That was Chris, trying to hush and comfort her. 'We thought you must have rumbled—well, got some sort of idea. If you'd asked we'd have told you. We were going to anyway, in the next week or so. We were going to tell you, but we thought you were more than half prepared, and then we'd all go and break it to Leo.'

Robina stared at the drawing room door, and she could almost see the man in that room, and she asked dully, 'Who breaks it to him now?'

'We'll come down tomorrow, we'll be with you by mid-day,' Chris promised, but that was a long time away.

'What do I tell him *now*?'

'You might say,' said Chris, 'that Sarah and I love each other very much, and we're getting married right away, and we'd like him to be happy for us. But if he isn't that's just too bad.'

'Is it?' Robina imagined herself walking in there and say-ing that, but she couldn't imagine getting a very sym-pathetic hearing from Leo Morgan.

'I'm sorry, love,' said Chris. 'I didn't want you left down there with him on your own,' but Robina had taken in all she could take and her head was bursting. She said, 'I'll see you both tomorrow,' and put down the phone.

She went straight to the drawing room. There was no way thinking things over was going to help. Leo was stand-ing by the fireplace. He might have been smiling, but it wasn't a smile that made you feel better. 'Quite a long conversation,' he commented. 'She's with the artist?'

Robina got it out in a rush. 'You asked just now if you knew him. Well, it's Christopher, my brother, and they say they're getting married.'

The smile deepened, or rather the lines around his mouth did. 'I was considering that possibility.'

'You were? That it was Chris?'

'The Spanish affair is over. He's marrying the girl Sarah temporarily cut out.' Leo had a villa there, he could get discreet reports on anyone locally. With his money he could get discreet reports on anyone anywhere. 'Your brother is a personable young man who could loosely be described as an artist,' he went on. 'And it explains why you were pleading their cause.'

Ten minutes ago she hadn't known the man was Chris. Now she said, 'Well, he's got no money, but he's talented, and she could have made a worse choice.' He might agree with her, because it was true, but he said,

'You think so?'

At the moment she was feeling pretty sick with Chris, but usually she admired and loved him. She didn't put his chances of staying happily married to Sarah very high, but he wouldn't hurt her as her first husband had, he had said they loved each other. 'Chris loves her,' she said. 'She hopes you'll go on paying her allowance, but money doesn't matter to Chris.'

Leo threw back his head and roared with laugher, and Robina stared, then tried to shout the laughter down. 'It *doesn't*! Chris doesn't care about money. He's no—no opportunist.'

Leo's eyes were hard as flint, although his voice was soft. 'A thief is an opportunist of the most basic kind,' he said.

'A thief?' Robina tried to laugh herself. 'You mean he stole Sarah? Oh, come off it!'

'You come off it, Miss Jefferson late of Cliffe Castle.' And she cowered from the contempt that came at her with the force of a physical blow although the man hadn't moved. 'You know and I know we're talking about money. Cash. Embezzlement. This time Sarah has got herself a crook.'

CHAPTER SEVEN

'You must be out of your mind!' cried- Robina, but Leo went relentlessly on.

'My accountants discovered it when they went through the books. Small-time stuff, but hardly a character reference.'

He must be talking about the family firm. Chris must have dipped into the cash somehow while he was working there, and although she had always taken it for granted that her brother was scrupulously honest she had discovered tonight that there was a great deal she didn't know about him. 'You're sure it was Chris?' she asked, and Leo's look was answer enough. There was no doubt whatever, and she said unhappily, 'I didn't know. I had nothing to do with the business. I was going to run the Castle and Chris was supposed to be carrying on the firm, that was how it was always planned.'

She faltered at his cynical smile and ended desperately, 'Nor did I know Sarah was meeting Chris today. I thought it was still the Spanish boy. I'm a fool.'

She had only taken a few steps into the room, and she put a hand on the back of a chair steadying herself because her legs were still rubbery. 'Oh no,' said Leo, 'we're not going along with that assumption. You're no fool, you're a sharp girl, but you've conned me for the last time and so long as you understand that we might be able to deal with the problem.'

She hadn't 'conned' anybody, she was the one who had been duped, but she asked mechanically, 'Chris and Sarah?'

'Is there any other problem?'

She had problems of her own, but Leo wouldn't want to talk about them, so she said, 'I can't think of any. Would you mind if I sit down?'

The phone call had shaken and hurt her and being told that Chris had cheated Uncle Randolph came as a double blow, engulfing her in misery. She sat down, promising herself that she would soon be out of this. She was off tomorrow. Not tonight, because she felt like a wet rag, but tomorrow she was away.

'They're getting married?' Leo came and stood in front of her and she nodded. She had told him they had told her that. 'Well, we can't stop them, can we?'

Of course they couldn't stop them. Robina kept her head bowed and her eyes on her own clenched hands, but somehow she could still see his face, dark and watchful.

'You think the marriage would have a better chance if it was subsidised?' he asked, and she said slowly, 'I think Sarah would be happier.'

That was her honest opinion. Chris was usually broke and for most of her life Sarah had been a rich girl, but if it wasn't too tough for her it might work out, and it did seem that Leo was considering a helping hand.

'I might be prepared to pay up,' he said. 'With a surety.'

The only financial surety Robina could offer would be the Castle, if he was still interested in that, but she didn't feel over-generous towards Chris and Sarah at the moment. It was different for Leo. He was rolling in money and he always had felt responsible for Sarah. She said, 'They said they'd be here tomorrow about midday. I suppose we could phone them, I think they're at Chris's place, although I don't really know.'

'No need to spoil their night,' said Leo, and Robina turned her head sharply, looking away from him, demanding,

'What kind of surety? The Castle? Are you suggesting I help set them up in comfort?'

'That is the idea.'

She looked back then quickly enough, but the indignant retort died on her lips when Leo said, 'I'll go on paying Sarah's allowance, with possibly a slight increase, so long as you stay here.'

Her cheeks were scalding as he looked at her, because he had no scrap of respect, and probably very little liking for her. But the sexual pull was still there, the physical awareness; she said harshly, 'What do you want me for, resident lover?'

'If you insist,' he drawled, and anger choked her as he walked to a bureau that stood across the room and opened a drawer, apparently checking for something. Robina looked at his broad back—it was easier to talk to that than to his face—and asked, 'Why, then?'

'Your brother seems fond of you.' Chris was, nothing could alter that. 'If he remembers you're in my house it might influence the way he treats Sarah.'

He wanted her around as surety for Chris's good behaviour! He *must* be out of his mind!

'And there's a job for you here,' he went on. 'You work well with the staff, and I need a woman to welcome my guests and sit at the head of my table. I'm losing Sarah, I don't feel inclined to take a wife, and you fit the bill nicely.'

It showed how confused Robina was that her first reaction was that she did indeed fit the bill and she could cope very nicely with the job. She voiced the first objection that occurred to her. 'What will everyone think if Sarah leaves and I stay? What would they think my position was?'

Leo folded a couple of sheets of paper, then turned back to look at her and said flatly, 'Most of them will think we're lovers and none of them will give a damn.'

Nobody would care what she did, that was true. And they would not be lovers, but she asked, 'If I go you just leave them alone?'

'If you go,' he smiled as he spoke, 'I might let the news leak that anyone considering financial transactions with Christopher Jefferson should think again.'

'That would be slander, he could sue you,' but she knew that Chris wouldn't have a chance, that a word from Leo Morgan could finish her brother, and that Leo did not intend her to leave his house. She felt the trap closing in on her and she said through stiff lips, 'You don't want me here to arrange menus with Mrs Palmer and act as hostess. You want a whipping boy, someone to punish if Chris and Sarah hit a bad patch.'

He was still smiling. 'That sounds very masochistic.'

'I'm no masochist. Are you a sadist?' She was out of her chair, but although he was still over there by the bureau he seemed to be between her and the door too.

'You might find that out,' he said. 'And now, if you'll excuse me.' Robina shrank away as he passed her by and she stood quite still until he had crossed the hall and gone back into the study, then she ran like the wind up the stairs, and along the corridor into her bedroom. She shut the door and locked it.

She had no idea who she thought she was turning the key against. Leo wasn't following her and she couldn't imagine Mrs Palmer turning up for a chat, not after having gone through Robina's wastepaper basket for Sarah's note. But she wanted to keep everyone out. There was no one tonight she wanted to see, or she felt she could trust, and in here at least there was an illusion of safety. Unless the house set fire she need not come out till morning.

She would probably have spent a sleepless night, but there were sleeping pills that Dr Buxton had left after the Castle burned, and she swallowed a couple and slept dreamlessly, waking with a slight headache and heavy eyes. It was after ten o'clock, but no one had come near her, and as she dressed the phone rang, but if it was for her she wasn't called.

Downstairs she heard the hum of a vacuum cleaner, and in the breakfast room there was toast in the toast rack and hot coffee in the pot. She sat alone, drinking the coffee and playing with the toast. Gladys the daily help came in to clear away, and was cheery enough. She said good morning and wasn't it a nice day? and Robina wondered how much she knew and what would happen when she herself finally bumped into Mrs Palmer. That could be an awkward moment, but the hall was empty when she emerged from the breakfast room and went into the music room which overlooked the drive.

Until Chris and Sarah arrived she didn't really know what her next move was going to be. She supposed she wanted to wash her hands of them all, but of course she liked living here. And if she stayed she would be on the spot to see about Castle business, and she could always walk out later. No one could keep her anywhere against her will, and there was a legitimate job going. She would have to consider. There would have to be a conference.

The garage doors were closed, so she had no way of knowing if Leo was here or not. He could be coming back midday to 'chair' the conference, but she was almost sure he was still in the house. Twice, since she came downstairs, a phone had rung and stopped almost at once. If he was in the study they would have rung on his desk, whether they were business or home calls, and her nerve-ends told her he wasn't far away.

Not that that was anything to go by. The situation was tense, she was on edge, and it didn't necessarily have anything to do with Leo Morgan's physical presence. She put a record on the music centre, opening the door a few inches—that would warn everyone she was in here and probably keep them out, and it was something to do instead of just sitting. She was nervous as a cat, she couldn't sit still.

She had chosen at random, taking the first record that came to hand, which happened to be an Edith Piaf, and was standing at the window where she could see Chris and Sarah's car as it came down from the road when the 'little sparrow's' electrifying voice ran out with *Je ne regrette rien*.

Robina dashed back to the record player and turned it right down, because with her luck Leo would hear and decide that this was aimed at him. Why else would she be filling the house with a defiant cry that she regretted nothing she had done? It wasn't very subtle, but it was forceful, and perhaps turning it down in mid-song wasn't too tactful either. That rather emphasised the message.

Her lips twitched, in all this gloom she could have done with a laugh, and she went back to the window prepared for a long and lonely vigil. But almost at once Sarah's car appeared, with Chris at the wheel. They didn't see her. They got out of the car and walked towards the house arm in arm, talking earnestly to each other. Looking at them brought a lump to Robina's throat. She was annoyed with them, they had put her in a very awkward position, but she couldn't help hoping that things were going to turn out well for them.

She walked out of the music room as they came into the hall, and stood and waited as they hurried towards her. 'You okay?' Chris asked, his eyes searching her face.

'Why?' she demanded. 'Did you think Leo might have beaten me up when I broke your news?'

Sarah gave a gasp of laughter, but Chris's expression was set and serious. 'We phoned again last night,' he said, 'and got Leo. He said you'd gone to your room and couldn't be disturbed and he'd see us here at eleven.'

It was only half past ten. It seemed longer since she came downstairs, and they must have left London very early. She said tartly, 'And you came running to see him, so you're not planning on living on love?'

Sarah led the way into the drawing room. Her cheeks were flushed and her eyes were very bright. She held on to Chris and he said, 'I'm not making a fortune. I love Sarah, but I can't give her this kind of life.' Sarah was starting to speak, but he went right on, 'And I'm not Leo's ideal brother-in-law, am I?'

'No,' said Robina levelly, 'and not because you're a self-employed cameraman either.' She looked at Sarah and Sarah said quickly,

'Oh, I know all about that. Chris told me as soon as things started to get serious between us.'

'Nobody told me,' said Robina. 'Uncle Randolph never said a word about my brother dipping into the till. It was my night last night for surprises. I was quite surprised when Leo said that this time Sarah had got herself a thief.'

Chris flushed, looking, Robina thought, like a small boy caught out in some misdemeanour. And that was how he seemed to consider it. 'For God's sake, I didn't rob the Bank of England! I was bored out of my skull in that job and I borrowed enough to tide me over while I started up in something I did want to do. That was all. It was the family business, wasn't it, it owed me something. I didn't think it would even be noticed.'

'You didn't fiddle the books that well,' snapped Robina. 'Leo's accountants soon spotted it.'

That must have broken Uncle Randolph's spirit as much as losing the firm, that could have caused his tears, and Chris said raggedly, 'It was only a few thousand. I'm sorry about it, love, I've always been sorry about it, and then when I met Sarah it was another reason why Leo wasn't going to take to me. That was why we didn't want him finding out until he'd——' he hesitated and Robina said,

'Until he'd taken to me?' She was standing with folded arms and she gripped her fingers tighter, holding in the anger. 'Oh, he thinks I'm a lovely lady. That's why he doesn't want to let me go. I've been invited to stay on here.'

They both stared then Sarah said, almost timidly, 'Well, that's terrific. Isn't it?'

'Why?' asked Chris.

'I was trained to run the Castle. Instead I'll be helping to run this house. He's losing Sarah, and he needs a resident hostess.'

'Do you want to stay?' Chris met her glinting eyes and in his eyes was pleading and pain. It was no good railing at him because he had 'borrowed' from the old firm and fallen in love with a girl who looked like Marilyn Monroe.

Robina said tautly, 'It's very comfortable here. Where else could I find a job like this?'

'You could come to us,' Chris suggested. 'You'd soon find——'

'No, thank you.' She snapped out the words, and Leo came into the room and brought his own aura of power and command so that they were all silent, waiting for him to speak. He didn't. He looked at each face briefly, then seated himself, relaxed as a judge, and the three of them stood in a little group and Robina felt like one of the accused.

Sarah broke the silence. 'You know Chris.'

'Very well,' said Leo grimly, and Robina heard her brother gulp and saw him straighten his shoulders and felt sorry for him, trying to stand up to Leo.

'I don't have to ask you for Sarah's hand,' said Chris.

'You don't have to ask me for anything.' Leo's voice seemed deeper than ever, perhaps because nervousness was making Chris sound so young. 'But you're going to,' Leo went on, 'because you need the money. Your outfit is operating on a very tight budget.'

Since last night Robina knew that Leo had checked out Chris's finances so that he could probably give a run-down to the last pound. Chris didn't try to bluff. He said, 'All right, times are tough, but we'll manage,' and Sarah looked up at him adoringly.

'Chris loves me,' she told her brother, 'and we will manage, and you don't know him very well. It was silly, taking that money, and he did it on impulse and he's always regretted it. You know about that and you don't really know anything else about him, but you do know Robina.'

She took Robina's hand, she was already holding Chris's. 'You approve of her, don't you?' she asked Leo. 'And they're so alike.' A smile lifted the corners of her mouth. 'Love Robina, love Chris,' she said gaily, and Robina felt the chill of Leo's sardonic scrutiny.

'Quite a team,' he drawled. 'Sure you're not twins?'

They might have been, they looked so alike: the same dark hair and blue eyes, the pale oval face, and slim long-legged bodies. It was bitterly humiliating, standing here while Leo paired her off with Chris as someone who had tricked him and was now after his money. Love Robina, love Chris, indeed! Sarah should have said, 'Despise Chris, despise Robina.'

She wanted to pull her hand from Sarah's soft encircling fingers and tell Leo, 'I'm nothing like Chris. Under the skin we're as different as you and Sarah.' But it wouldn't have been true. Chris was her blood brother, and although Robina would never have taken that money they were alike in many ways. She had stayed at home while he had gone roaming, but in her heart of hearts she was as much a gipsy as he was. She couldn't disown Chris, she was linked with him, and right now she knew she was the stronger.

'We're not twins,' she said. 'Just brother and sister, like

you.' Leo always supported Sarah and she was supporting Chris, and suddenly Leo smiled, the attractive smile that Robina hadn't seen since last night. It could have been false for all she knew, but he looked friendly, and Sarah said in a rush, as though she wanted to catch him in this mood,

'We're getting married next month. Please come.'

'I'll be in America most of next month, but I'm sure Robina will be there. She can represent me.' He sounded amiable, he didn't sound as though there was any sarcasm in this. 'I'm sure she's told you,' he added, 'that I'll make an allowance to the pair of you so long as she's working for me.'

She hadn't reached the stage of telling them their allowance depended on her when Leo had walked in, so that was a surprise for them which made a change. They both looked puzzled. They didn't know whether to smile or not, whether he was joking or not, and Robina decided not to mention the real crux of the blackmail—that if she didn't stay not only would he not pay but he might, just possibly, leak the news of the doctored accounts.

She was staying, for now, and there was no sense starting on a bitter note. 'I'd love to come to the wedding and I hope you'll be very happy,' she said, and Sarah flung her arms around Robina's neck exclaiming,

'Oh, I'm so lucky to be getting you for my sister!'

'We're all lucky in Robina,' said Leo gravely, and that was sarcasm. She felt the flick of it, and met his eyes as Sarah hugged her, telling her,

'I hope you'll be happy too.'

'So do I,' said Robina, but she did not think that happiness was what Leo had in store for her.

'Can we stay tonight?' Sarah was beaming now, everything was fine.

'Of course,' said Leo.

'Can we tell Mrs P.?'

'Why not?' shrugged Leo.

Sarah opened the door and this time Mrs Palmer was in the hall, fiddling with a bowl of flowers that didn't need re-arranging. Unless they had gone out through the window they wouldn't have left this house without meeting Mrs Palmer. Sarah's smiles must have reassured her, because she came smiling into the room when Sarah called, 'Come and meet my young man.'

There was more hugging. Mrs Palmer thought that Chris was an improvement on Sarah's previous men, and Leo wasn't raising any objections to them getting married so soon, so Mrs Palmer hugged Sarah and then Chris; and when Sarah and Chris had gone off to find Jack and break the news to him she turned to Robina.

'I was that worried,' she said apologetically. 'That's why I hunted for that note. We've had some rare old do's with her, and I didn't know where she was off to this time. I didn't know it was your brother.' She didn't hug Robina, but she gave her a very approving look. 'He's got to be a good lad. Will they be living here?'

'No,' said Leo.

'Chris has a house in London,' Robina told her. 'Well, the top floor of a house.' Leo had a London house too, but there would be a big difference in the two establishments and she wondered if Sarah would be tempted to go round to her earlier home and wallow in luxury sometimes.

'It's a pity we'll be losing you,' said Mrs Palmer. 'I was coming to rely on you.'

She might just have been saying that, but when Leo told her, 'Robina will be staying with us,' she seemed genuinely pleased.

'Oh, I am glad,' she said, head on one side, bright eyes darting from Leo to Robina, waiting for further explanation. Robina waited too and Leo said,

'Sarah won't be needing a companion any more, so

Robina is going to act as my social secretary.'

Robina shrugged. One title was as good as another. To most folk she would be Leo's live-in lady no matter how often she stressed the platonic nature of the set-up, and her shoulders tensed as he put an arm around her. The gesture seemed to satisfy Mrs Palmer. She gave them a happy little nod and asked, 'Everybody in for lunch?'

'Just the family,' said Leo.

As the door closed after Mrs Palmer Robina stepped away. She was furious with herself because Leo's touch gave her the shakes inside. Just his hand on her shoulder could churn her up, and she glared at him, demanding, 'Why did you do that?'

'It's easier to let her think you're staying because we want to be together than explaining that you're a hostage.'

'This hostage can walk out,' she said crisply.

'So she can,' he agreed.

'And I wouldn't mind some insurance that Sarah is going to make Chris happy. She's been spoiled rotten, which is more than he has.'

'Well, they make a pretty pair,' said Leo cheerfully, and Robina felt that he was laughing at her. She supposed she shouldn't mind that, it must mean he was reassured about their chances of happiness. 'Let's hope Mrs P. is right and he is a good lad.'

'Oh, he is.' Chris had a touch of wildness in him, but when they were children Robina had always been the leader. 'Don't worry about Chris,' she said. But he needn't expect her to play her part meekly. 'I'm the one who could surprise you. You don't know what you're getting.'

His eyes narrowed almost imperceptibly, and his mouth tightened, slightly, but the effect was a little frightening. Then he said, 'You are the one who doesn't know. See you at lunch,' and left her.

Nothing surprised him, not even Chris and Sarah. He'd

worked that out before anyone told him. Before she left
this house she'd get herself baked in a pie and jump out in
the middle of a dinner party stark naked, and see if that
would leave him at a loss for words. She laughed softly,
recognised it as a nervous giggle, and swished around the
room, plumping up cushions and telling herself to calm
down.

A few minutes later Sarah walked in alone. 'Chris and
Tommy are having a natter about cars,' she said. 'Everything's working out beautifully, isn't it?'

'Beautifully,' Robina echoed, thinking that the 'working'
hadn't started yet. The problems still waited. She smoothed
a cushion and placed it on the back of the sofa, and Sarah
sat down on the sofa and smiled up at her and said,

'You will come to us sometimes, won't you? But I'm glad
you're staying here. You're just what Leo needs. You'll do
the hostessing far better than I ever could. I always told
you he goes for cool elegant ladies.'

'Well, you certainly dressed me for the part,' said Robina
drily.

'Well, it worked, didn't it?' Sarah had that pleased-with-
herself look. 'And it's true, isn't it? You are cool and
elegant.'

She was so confident that Robina would agree that when
Robina said, 'No, I'm not, I just look this way,' her smile
vanished. Robina was still dressed in clothes that were the
height of discreet good taste, but something in her stance
or her voice disconcerted Sarah, who stared, then blinked,
then said in very different tones from her teasing banter,
'Look, about Leo, can I give you a word of advice?'

'Of course.' Robina was not promising to follow Sarah's
suggestions, but Sarah was at liberty to voice them, and
she did so hesitantly, choosing her words.

'You know what you said about standing up to him?
Well, that's all right usually because he'll usually listen to

somebody else's point of view. But if you ever have a real row you'll have to do the apologising. He wouldn't know how to be humble.'

'I believe you,' said Robina, and laughed. 'But if we have a real row we'll be parting by mutual consent. This is just a job, it isn't going to turn into a love affair.'

'Oh!' Sarah seemed disappointed. 'Well, I suppose you should know, but I thought as you got on so well together——'

'No way,' said Robina.

'It would have been nice,' Sarah said wistfully, and Robina thought, No, it wouldn't. It would have been heaven and hell, and brief. It couldn't have lasted, and I am not putting myself any deeper into Leo Morgan's power.

The phone rang and stopped ringing, and Chris opened the door and said, to Sarah, 'It's for you. Your favourite gossip columnist.'

'Yeuk!' groaned Sarah, but she went to the hall table and picked up the phone, while Chris explained to Robina, 'We told a few folk last night.' So it was now general knowledge that Sarah Morgan was marrying Christopher Jefferson, and Sarah's clear voice reached them, answering questions.

'Yes, that's right, on the fifteenth of next month ... Oh, we've known each other ages, we sort of lived next door to each other. Chris's home was Cliffe Castle just across the bay from this house ... It burned down, yes, and Robina, his sister, has been staying here. Actually Leo's asked her to stay on, but I shall be coming back to London, of course.' She giggled at the next question. 'You'd better ask her, hadn't you?'

She held out the phone towards Robina, who shook her head violently. 'But not now,' said Sarah. 'She isn't here just now.'

'I'll go and help with the lunch,' said Robina. As she passed Sarah the girl was saying, 'Of course Leo approves. He's absolutely delighted.'

In the kitchen Mrs Palmer and Gladys wanted to know where the wedding was going to be. 'Because if it's here,' said Mrs Palmer, chopping chives vigorously, 'it isn't giving us much time, is it?'

Robina visualised Chris and Sarah slipping into a register office with a few friends, and then back to the flat for a noisy cheerful party. But she had to admit that she really hadn't a clue.

The phone kept ringing all morning, mostly for Sarah and Chris. Leo had gone over to the factory and Robina busied herself in the kitchen and around the house. But they all sat down for lunch at half past one, and almost the first thing Sarah said was, 'Everyone keeps asking where we're getting married. Can we have the reception here? I mean, this is my home, isn't it? I'd like to get married from home, in the little church.' Her eyes were fixed pleadingly on her brother. 'And I do wish you could be there. I don't want it to be like the last time.'

An elopement and a register office and a short and bitter marriage, and Robina said before she could stop herself, 'There'll be one big difference—the man. I shouldn't think your first husband and Chris have much in common.'

'By all means have it here,' said Leo. 'But I have to be in America, and Christopher should be all the support you'll need.'

Sarah grimaced, and Chris and Leo exchanged wry masculine glances, and Robina realised that her defence of Chris had been unnecessary. Both men knew that Sarah was trying to wheedle her own way, she wanted Leo at the wedding, but the look she turned on Chris was bright and loving.

Leo gave them carte blanche, which meant that he was

prepared to meet the bills, and the meal ended with Sarah making lists of guests. 'I can send the invitations off myself,' she said, 'if Robina will see about the reception arrangements. I'm going back with Chris tomorrow and I'll be coming down again a day or two before the wedding. We can get a special licence, can't we, so I don't actually have to be living here?'

Robina wondered if Leo was going to object, but all he said was, 'I'm sure Robina can cope, and Mrs P. will expect to be consulted.' Then he drained his coffee cup and looked at his watch, and said he would be back tonight about nine.

When he had gone Sarah smiled at both Chris and Robina. 'I didn't think I'd get away with that. I thought he'd say, "You stay here until the wedding".' She tried to mimic Leo's deep voice. ' "Let's have you behaving like a respectable woman for once". Didn't you think that?' she asked Robina, but Chris answered,

'No I didn't. He's letting you go off with me so that you'll get some idea what living with me is going to be like.'

Why not, thought Robina? Even a few weeks might be long enough to show if this romance was strong enough for a lifetime's committal.

'I know what it's going to be like,' said Sarah, starry-eyed. 'It's going to be super. And Leo's glad about us, you know. He likes you. And you like him, don't you?'

'Sure I like him,' said Chris, playing with his coffee spoon. 'And I admire him and I respect him.' He dipped the spoon in the brown granules and let the sugar trickle slowly into his cup. 'He doesn't admire me and he doesn't respect me, but I hope he likes me, because he is a very tough customer.' He looked at Robina. 'And I'd be happier if you were leaving here.'

She made herself smile. 'You heard what he said. He won't pay your allowance if I don't stay.'

'I heard,' said Chris. 'And I keep asking myself—why

is he so determined to keep you here, and what return does he expect for his money?'

There was quite a party that night. Sarah was off to London tomorrow, so everybody who wanted to hear more details about the wedding came round. The affair had been such a well-kept secret that they all thought this was another of Sarah's impulsive whims, and as the man was Robina Jefferson's brother and Robina had been living with the Morgans since the night of the fire they concluded that Robina had been matchmaking.

Chris had charm. He looked handsome and he was amusing and intelligent, and proud and protective of Sarah. They looked so well together and all the visitors congratulated them, and it was all smiles and handshakes until the callers moved away from the young couple. As soon as people were out of earshot, talking softly among themselves, they became much more cynical about the future for Sarah and her fiancé.

Robina saw the way they looked at each other, she heard some of their comments. A man said, 'I'll give it six months,' and a girl, realising that Robina was near, tried to be tactful: 'Yes, I know that's how long the last one lasted, but Chris seems a super chap.'

'Thank you,' said Robina ironically.

She was busy, serving drinks and the trays of 'bites' that Mrs Palmer was sending in from the kitchen. She was determined to work at this impromptu party to show Chris that she was staying here to do a genuine job. There had been almost a row after lunch, when Chris had asked Robina what Leo was expecting for his money.

Sarah had sat silent between them while Robina snapped, 'He's getting a hostess because he needs one and you're taking Sarah away, and he isn't a marrying man.'

'I'll bet he isn't,' Chris had snapped back. 'He doesn't marry 'em, but he has 'em, doesn't he? And I don't like the thought of my sister shacked up here.'

'Ha!' Robina had given a derisive hoot. 'That's rich, coming from a man who's been sharing beds ever since he got himself a roof.' She shouldn't have said that in front of Sarah, although Sarah must know about Laura and probably about the girls who had gone before.

'That's different,' said Chris infuriatingly, and Robina said,

'Well, it would be, wouldn't it?' But she knew Chris meant that his affairs had never been serious, no one had been hurt. He was afraid that Robina would be hurt if she became Leo's mistress, and he was feeling guilty that she might be staying here because of him.

He said, 'Don't feel you've got to do this for us, we can manage without the allowance,' and Robina said very slowly, her voice rising with exasperation,

'It's a job, like a secretary or a cook. If you think Leo's going to seduce me as soon as he has a spare half hour you'd better tell him, hadn't you, that if he makes any passes he'll have you to answer to?' '

'Oh, *Chris*!' Sarah's gurgle of laughter had made Chris smile wryly. The idea of him scaring Leo was ridiculous, it made Robina giggle too, and there they were, the three of them, rolling around in their chairs laughing. But tonight Robina was very much the busy hostess, attending to the guests.

She wasn't enjoying herself much. The change in atmosphere, as you walked away from the warm circle round Chris and Sarah, was like a sharp drop in temperature. On the fringe of the circle the smiles began to falter, faces sobered, and by the time you were skirting the wall you couldn't hear an optimistic word.

Not unless they noticed you. When they saw Robina they smiled again and became quite animated until she turned her back. She saw that happen in a mirror; three women beamed at her and said how exciting it all was, and how happy they just knew that Sarah was going to be, and the moment Robina had passed by with her tray the smiles dropped from their faces like masks.

Her worst moment came when she was stacking plates on a side table, head bowed, not very noticeable, and somewhere near she heard a woman say softly, 'Of course they don't have any money. The old man died broke, and the Castle wasn't insured, so this will be a very good thing for them.' The implication was that Chris and Robina were a couple on the make, and anger rose in Robina.

She stepped round the man who had blocked her from view and faced the woman, who had been a visitor to Cliffe Castle in the old days but not when the hard times came. 'Hello, Mrs Littleton,' she said gaily, 'I thought I recognised your voice. Having fun?' She smiled a cool amused smile, and watched a flush of embarrassment blotch Mrs Littleton's face, then she moved on, still smiling.

But inside she felt resentful, although she could understand their misgivings. This announcement was a bolt from the blue. Some of these people had thought they were in Sarah's confidence but she hadn't breathed a word to any of them about Chris Jefferson. It was all very fishy, and Mrs Littleton wasn't the only one who suspected that Sarah was being hustled into marriage by another fortune hunter.

Robina went into the kitchen, where Mrs Palmer was arranging a further supply of bite-sized sandwiches on a big oval dish, and Jack was reading the evening paper. Jack had trained himself to shut out kitchen activities when he was off duty, and he held up the paper like a shield, slowly assimilating the sports page.

'Shall I take these in?' Mrs Palmer stood back from her plate.

'Please,' said Robina, 'I'm going out for some air.'

Jack peered round his paper, hearing Robina's voice,

and said, 'Don't blame you, I reckon we've got half the county here.'

All afternoon Sarah had been inviting her phone callers to come round for a celebration drink tonight, and it seemed that everyone had. 'Some of them know Chris already,' said Robina. 'They can't all have come to get a look at Chris,' and Mrs Palmer suggested,

'Perhaps they're here to see the master.'

'He should be here by now, he said he'd be home by nine.' Robina added tartly, 'Do they think he's going to stop the wedding?'

'They could be waiting to see how he's taking it before they buy the presents,' Mrs Palmer chuckled, picking up the dish of sandwiches, and Robina smiled because Mrs Palmer was having her little joke. But Sarah was notorious for picking the wrong man and Leo had laid down the law more than once. Probably some of the visitors would be quite pleased if he brought an undercurrent of displeasure to the party. It would give them something else to gossip about when they left, and by the looks of it they weren't leaving until he came.

There were rows of cars lining the drive and filling most of the space in front of the garages. Robina heard the sound of yet another arriving as she came outside and she walked away from them all, through the gardens as far as she could go without taking the steps down to the beach. There was a little wooden bench here, and a low white fence gave warning of the cliff's edge.

Surely nothing in the world was more beautiful than the sea at night when the moon was high. On a still summer's night, like this, just looking at it could calm you so that the snubs and the sneers fell into proportion as something that didn't matter much. No one would miss her for a few minutes and she sat down, leaning forward, resting arms and chin on the top rail of the fence, and imagined herself floating out over the shimmering water.

It was only a few minutes and she was thinking, All right, that's it, back to the party, when she heard Leo calling. Another minute and she would have been walking back to the house, but she still felt piqued at being disturbed. It irritated her, hearing him shouting, 'Bina, where are you?' Not that he was shouting. The night was still and the words carried.

She said, 'Here,' and she didn't get up because she had earned a rest. He must have walked straight into the house, checked that the hostess was not hostessing, and come looking for her. He had almost found her before he called her name, because almost at once he was by the bench.

He sat down beside her and asked, 'What are you doing out here?'

'Getting a breather,' she said. 'That's quite a crowd.' She couldn't see his expression clearly, but he laughed, so he hadn't come looking for her to complain.

'It's a full house all right,' he agreed. 'How many has she invited?'

'Everybody who phoned up this afternoon, and the phone never stopped ringing.'

'Do you mind if I smoke?'

'Of course not.'

Leo took a cigar out of his pocket, lit and drew on it, and when the aroma of cigar smoke mixed with the scent of the flowers and the smell of the sea Robina breathed deeply and Leo asked, 'Why the sigh? Am I intruding?'

'I wasn't sighing.' And he wasn't intruding, although a few moments before she had resented not being left alone. Now he was sitting beside her she didn't mind him being here. She said, 'I'm sniffing the air. The sea and the garden and your cigar, it's an intriguing combination. If someone could bottle it they could have a real——' she was going to say 'aphrodisiac,' but she changed that to 'best-seller.'

'And the scent of your hair,' he said.

There was always a little breeze here, on the cliff's edge. Tonight it did no more than stir the heavy waves of her hair, but when he said that she expected him to reach and touch. The image was so vivid that she could feel the pressure on her temples, the fingertips, cool and firm and caressing, sliding down the nape of her neck, down her spine.

She shifted uneasily although he hadn't moved, and began to talk quickly. 'If Sarah issues invitations like this in London she'll fill Chris's flat twice over.' That sounded as though Chris was taking Sarah to a bed-sitter, and she continued, 'Not that it's that small, Chris's place. He's lucky really, he's got the whole of the top floor and it's a rambling sort of house.'

'It sounds charming,' said Leo, but she doubted if he meant that. She said, 'Mrs Palmer thinks they've come to see you.'

'Why me?'

'To see how you're taking it. It was a surprise announcement and if you disapprove that makes it even more interesting.'

'Well, I'm always sorry to disappoint my guests, but even if I did disapprove they wouldn't know.' He was smiling and he had said 'even if', which could mean that he was less anti-Chris than he had been at the beginning.

Robina had been about to go back into the house, but now she was reluctant to move. It was peaceful out here and the silence between them was an easy one. She felt she could have sat for hours without straining for something to say, quiet and content.

The sounds from the house reached them, but the sigh-

ing of the sea was a soporific music and although Leo
didn't touch her the companionship of his presence was
like a strong gentle arm around her.

Moonlight silvered everything. Across the bay it glinted
on the pale stonework of the Castle and she asked him,
'Do you want the Castle? Are you going to buy it?'

'Yes.'

That was a relief. It meant that she would have something left. Not a home but a little money. She said, 'I'm
glad it's not going to end as a ruin, but inside it will be
changed completely, won't it?'

'Fairly radically,' he agreed, and after a moment he
added, 'But you don't have to give up all of it.'

'What do you mean?' she asked.

'You could keep on an apartment. Perhaps including the
small drawing room. That wasn't badly burned, it could
be restored without much trouble.'

Her eyes filled with tears as though someone had given
her a wonderful and unexpected gift, because the Castle
had always been part of her life. She wanted to travel, see
the world, but it would mean so much to know that she
could still come home to the Castle. The small drawing
room was a biggish room, and it had almost escaped the
fire. She could replace the furniture, or select from the rest
that was salvaged. She began to plan, and Leo said, 'Well?'

'Oh *yes*! I never thought about asking if I could keep a
bit.' She hadn't thought she could make conditions. He
was the only buyer, and the reconstruction plans had
covered the entire building. She told him, 'I'd like to keep
it like it used to be. Everything's filthy, of course, I don't
know about the wallpaper, I wonder——'

He laughed at her bubbling enthusiasm. 'We'll get it
matched.'

'Thank you.'

'And now we'd better be getting back.'

When Leo Morgan walked into the room with Robina that gave the guests something else to think about. The news was already around that Robina was staying on here, and Leo's hand on her arm was noted. So that was how it was. No wonder he had no objections to Christopher Jefferson!

One girl took it on herself to warn Robina that Leo was still seeing Imogen Faulkner. She was the one who had said earlier that Chris seemed a 'super chap', she might have thought this was a kindness too. She was among the late leavers and Robina was outside, helping to guide out the cars, when Fiona darted across and blurted, 'Look, I think I ought to tell you that he's still seeing Imogen.'

'What?'

Lights were flashing all around and somebody was backing out none too expertly and Robina had heard exactly what Fiona was saying.

'Leo,' hissed Fiona. 'Imogen. If you're staying here as his live-in lady I thought you ought to know.'

'I'm not——' Robina began. 'Hard down left!' she shouted, as the Datsun she was directing narrowly missed side-swiping a Rover. 'It's none of my business,' she said to Fiona.

'No?' said Fiona. 'Well, you'll be where he can find you, won't you? He won't have to go looking for you.'

Both Sarah and Mrs Palmer tried to persuade Robina not to bother with the clearing-up. Sarah was yawning, it had been a long day for her, and when she saw Robina putting glasses on a tray she said, 'Oh, *leave* it, you've been on your feet all night.'

'Yes, you go on up,' Mrs Palmer added her persuasion. 'This won't take more than half an hour in the morning and Gladys'll be here then.'

'But I'm not tired,' Robina protested, 'so I will just stack the dishwasher. You all go to bed, you'll probably be up before me.'

There was no sign of Leo, and Sarah and Chris said goodnight and climbed the stairs, ostensibly to their separate rooms. And Mrs Palmer, after checking that all was in order in the breakfast room, went off to join Jack who had been fast asleep in bed, and snoring, for the past hour.

It wasn't late. It wasn't midnight yet, and Robina was sure that she wouldn't fall asleep easily. She didn't want to take pills again, but her nerves felt as tense and tight as an overwound watch.

There wasn't really much to do down here. Just glasses and ashtrays to carry into the kitchen, and a few chairs to put back in place. She moved quickly, breathing shallowly, and catching sight of herself in the mirror stopped to stare. She hadn't realised how angry she was until she saw how she was scowling now that she was alone.

Fiona had made her so furious that she had wanted to scream. Not for telling her about Leo and Imogen, of course, but the cool way she took it for granted that Robina was just another of Leo's mistresses. It was so insulting. That was why Robina felt now that she wanted to throw something hard at the wall, smash something up, burst into tears. Although why she was in this state goodness knows, because what did it matter what Fiona thought?

But she would probably be taking the pills again tonight because she felt that only a knock-out draught could calm her down. Or she might try listening to a little music, something nostalgic and soothing, and sit quietly in a deep soft chair for a while before she went upstairs. That might help; it could hardly do any harm.

There was a light still on in the music room. When

Robina opened the door she heard music playing and as she walked across the room she saw Leo in one of the armchairs. She gave a yelp of alarm, and gasped, 'I didn't know there was anyone in here.' She couldn't hang around now. 'I was doing a final check-up.'

'Not coming back to play Piaf again?' He smiled at her and she forced a little laugh.

'It did rather blare out, didn't it? But I didn't choose it for the message.'

'Do you like Chopin?' So that was what was playing. She listened for a moment, and nodded,

'Yes, but I think I'll be getting to bed. Everyone else has.'

Leo got up out of the chair and the walls of the room seemed to be closing in on her. She wanted to push them out, and push him away if he came any closer. 'May I come to your room tonight?' he asked, and something exploded in her head.

The expression about 'blowing your top' was right. The suppressed anger whooshed through her, and words erupted as though a safety valve had blown. She didn't stop to think what she was saying, she didn't have time. The words were tumbling over themselves with hardly a breath between so that she seemed to be listening rather than speaking.

No, he could not come to her room. Sex was not part of the service, and if it was a condition on his buying the Castle and keeping up Sarah's allowance and forgetting that Chris had borrowed from the family firm she could tell him what he could do with his whole package deal. She did tell him, in detail. She also told him that if he ever came near her after the hours of darkness she would scream so loud they'd hear her for miles and who the hell did he think he was, what did he think he was, to think she was here for his taking?

She had never rounded on anyone like this in her life, never felt so insulted before. The words tasted bitter on her tongue, making nausea rise in her throat. She could have heaved, thrown up, and she clenched her teeth and practically snarled, 'Have you got that? Has the message penetrated? Have I made myself clear?'

'As crystal.' The deep slow drawl sounded like a soothing doctor with an hysterical patient, or like a man holding back a smile. 'But a simple no would have been sufficient.'

Robina felt in a state of complete disarray, as though her hair must be standing on end with crackling fury, but Leo was calm, immaculate from head to foot and almost smiling, and the indignation began to ebb out of her. She had made a right spectacle of herself, carrying on as though he was proposing raping her, when all she had needed to do was say 'No, thank you', coolly and cheerfully.

They were consenting adults and he had presumed she was of average experience, able to deal with a civilised pass without going into the screaming hab-dabs. He must think nobody had ever fancied her before from the way she had reacted.

'Sorry,' she said, 'I think I drank too much.' She had hardly drunk anything, she had just handed the drinks round, but she had to find some excuse, she had to explain in some way and get out of here. 'Goodnight,' she said.

'Goodnight,' he was amused not annoyed, when she scurried out of the room. He would listen to Chopin a little longer and then go up to his room and go to sleep. If she had said 'Yes' he would have made love to her, with skill and consideration, and it would have been a pleasant hour or so for him. But her refusal was no real deprivation. Asking her was an afterthought. If she hadn't walked into the music room he wouldn't have asked, and he would never come uninvited. She was very sure now of that.

Once she had thought he would. She had believed that

the physical attraction between them was so strong that it would sweep them together without any need for words, and perhaps it had been for her. But not for him.

She reached her room and got herself ready for bed. Her pride had been hurt. That was why she had lost her head and her sense of humour, and carried on like somebody demented. Leo was still seeing Imogen Faulkner, by which Fiona meant that he was still sleeping with her, and it was no compliment to be propositioned because your bed was the handier.

All the same a brief 'No' should have been enough, and she lay in the darkness despising herself. And not only because of the silly scene she had thrown just now, but because in her heart she knew how much she had wanted to tell Leo that he could come to her room tonight.

CHAPTER EIGHT

LEO had left the house before Chris and Sarah and Robina sat down to breakfast. When Robina came down Chris and Sarah had the morning paper spread out on the table, and Chris turned it towards Robina's chair while Sarah reached for the teapot to pour her a cup of tea.

There was a good photograph of Sarah, taken at a party, holding a champagne glass and smiling at someone who was out of the picture, and a small unsmiling one of Leo. Sarah had the caption 'To Wed', and Leo had 'Delighted'.

'Keeping it in the family . . .' Robina read, 'Tycoon Leo Morgan and blonde twenty-one-year-old sister Sarah are pairing off with brother and sister Christopher and Robina Jefferson, their next door neighbours until a fire destroyed Cliffe Castle, Cornwall, a few weeks ago. Since then Robina has been living with the Morgans and she plans to stay on and keep Leo company when Sarah leaves home to marry Chris next month. Leo is delighted at his sister's choice of a husband, although readers of this column will remember that some of her earlier very-good-friends did not meet with fraternal approval.'

It went on to recap a few of Sarah's escapades, mentioned the title of Chris's last TV film, and gave a string of companies that Leo controlled. Robina skimmed the lines and asked, 'Did he say he was delighted?'

'I told them that,' said Sarah, and Chris muttered, 'He looks about as delighted as Attila the Hun. Bloody cheek, isn't it? Bloody rubbish! They've no right to pair you off like this.'

Leo might be annoyed, but Imogen would be livid and

163

Robina stifled a grin. 'Oh, take no notice. Sarah's had this sort of thing before, haven't you? Don't fuss about it.'

'That's what I've been telling him,' said Sarah. She folded the newspaper and tossed it aside and Chris demanded,

'How long *are* you staying here?'

'Until the wedding anyway,' said Robina. 'Somebody's got to arrange things this end,' and after that they drifted into wedding talk. The number of probable guests was left with Mrs Palmer, who knew which caterers to contact, and as soon as breakfast was over Chris and Sarah said goodbye. They both held on to Robina, as though they weren't too sure about leaving her behind, and as Chris switched on the ignition he was still reminding her that there was plenty of room for her with them.

She went on waving until the car vanished at the top of the drive and when she came back into the house the phone was ringing. She had taken two calls over breakfast from people who had read the gossip column. She was even being asked if it was going to be a double wedding and that wasn't funny.

'There's not a word of truth in it,' she protested. 'I'm going back to live in the Castle when it's restored, and Leo has said I can stay on here and help Mrs Palmer the housekeeper till then. But there's nothing between Leo and me. Absolutely nothing.'

This time it was an old school friend who had written when Uncle Randolph died, inviting her to come and stay, and once Robina had explained again that the 'scoop' was pure fantasy, she wasn't having an affair with a millionaire, Margaret repeated her offer.

'Any time,' said Margaret, who was married to a farmer in Wiltshire, 'for as long as you like. You know I'd love to see you again.'

The next call was from another newspaper and Robina

told them too that she and Leo were friends, no more, and decided that she couldn't go on like this all day. 'Would you mind if I cleared off for a few hours?' she asked Mrs Palmer. 'Would you mind being left with the telephone?'

'Leave them to me,' said Mrs Palmer grimly. 'I know what to say to them, whoever they are.' She had had experience of harassment by phone during Sarah's troubles. 'No comment,' she said, and Robina wondered if that wasn't going to make everybody convinced that something was going on.

She got into her car and went along the coast, stopping at a popular resort and mixing with the crowds. She bought herself some new clothes, all in a much cheaper range than the garments Sarah had helped to select. Jeans for a start and a cotton skirt and several tops, and a bright red dress because she was in revolt from the muted shades that Sarah had chosen with Leo in mind. So he preferred cool elegant ladies, but Robina was dressing to please herself from now on, and even when her finances were settled she was never going to be rich. The couture names were out for her, but her long legs and slim hips had always looked good in jeans, and she changed in the changing room and ate in a snack bar, and all the holidaymakers around made her feel that she was on a day's holiday herself.

During the afternoon she looked in on the Castle. The demolition gang were still at work and the foreman came across when her car drew up, just as he had the day before yesterday. But this time he said, 'We saw the bit about your brother and Miss Morgan.' He didn't add, 'And about you and the boss,' but his grin widened and Robina said,

'Yes, everyone's very happy for them. I want to look at one of the rooms I'm thinking of keeping on here,' and she went through the cavern of the hall into the small drawing room.

There was a downstairs cloakroom practically adjoining,

and it would be easy to make a little kitchenette. This room was dirty, with smoke from the fire and dust from the demolition, but it could be put back almost the way it was. When she got back to Leo's house she would make a list of the furniture she was going to need, and when she was feeling low she would think about this room again and know that it wasn't a dream it really was waiting for her.

She came out smiling and felt all eyes on her. While she was Miss Jefferson they had felt sorry for her, she seemed a nice girl and the fire was a bad business, but since they'd read this morning's paper she had become much more glamorous and important.

The foreman walked back to her Mini with her, asking what she wanted doing about the drawing room, and she wondered whether to tell him not to believe everything he read in the papers. But she was sure that Leo would be issuing denials soon enough. The next time she came over here they'd be nice to her, they always were, but she wouldn't get the VIP treatment she was receiving as 'Leo Morgan's bird'.

It was all rather a joke, she could see the funny side of it, although Chris hadn't and she didn't suppose that Leo would. She hoped Leo would come home late so that she need only see him for a little while, because facing him again was going to be embarrassing enough after last night without this newspaper story on top of it.

But Mrs Palmer was expecting him home for dinner, so Robina changed out of her jeans into her red dress and helped in the kitchen, then sat in the drawing room with the list of those who had tried to phone her today. Some were friends whom she should contact, some she didn't know at all; and she was wondering what she could say to the friends when Leo walked in.

Her breath caught for a moment, then she relaxed because he relaxed as he sat down. He leaned back in the big armchair with a sigh of satisfaction and smiled at her. 'They got off all right?'

'Just after breakfast.' If people had been phoning her about the report they would certainly have been phoning him, and she had to know what he was doing about it. She said, 'You saw the paper, of course?'

'Is it worrying you?'

'Well, no, not much.' Not as much as she had thought it would bother him. 'But shouldn't we deny it? Ask them to print a retraction or something?'

'Far better leave it alone,' said Leo. 'Don't stir it on a gossip column. Let them print what they like, nobody remembers what went in last week.'

'All right, you've had more experience with them than me,' she said, and then remembered that most of his experience had been the stories printed about Sarah, and he couldn't enjoy thinking about them.

She and Uncle Randolph had read them and thought it was all a joke. 'What's our little china doll up to now?' he would say when Sarah's picture smiled up at them. The last time, the Spanish story, Sarah was already involved with Chris. Uncle Randolph wouldn't have believed that, just as he wouldn't believe that Robina could be here like this with Leo Morgan. He would have been afraid for her because the power of 'the pirate' had always frightened him.

'No gentleman,' he had called Leo, but Leo Morgan had style as well as strength. A more impressive man would be hard, if not impossible to find. I admire him, thought Robina, and we are friends, and that's the best way, because I could never compete with Imogen and the rest of them.

She said, 'About last night, I'm sorry I screeched.'

'It won't happen again,' he shrugged, and she believed him. He must have thought her painfully naïve, but the vehemence of her response had shown how scared she was of letting him make love to her. He wasn't likely to risk another bout of hysterics. No man wanted a woman under his roof screaming 'Rape!' She was safe enough now, and as soon as the wedding was over she would start looking around for somewhere else to live until her apartment in the Castle was ready.

In the meantime she gave herself unstintingly, in every way but physical intimacy. Preparing for a society wedding in just over four weeks was quite a task. The reception was being held in the house and gardens. There would be marquees on the lawns, and there was the food and the music, and some rather spectacular lighting and floral decorations to arrange, and it seemed sad that Sarah was missing the fun of the planning. But Sarah was determined not to come back until the day before the wedding.

She and Chris phoned often. He was working near his home and Sarah was going around with the team, and she always sounded happy when she talked to Robina, and thrilled about everything that was being laid on for the wedding.

Most of the invited guests replied to Sarah at Chris's address. When the acceptances came Sarah told Robina and Robina ticked them off on the list that Sarah had left behind. Imogen's name had to be added, it wasn't on the original list. 'She's sent us a present,' Sarah explained. 'A lovely little silver tray, so we had to ask her.'

'Of course you did,' Robina agreed, and wrote 'Imogen Faulkner' so hard that the ballpoint stabbed through the paper.

'By the way, has she been down?' Sarah's query was elaborately offhand.

'No,' said Robina, equally casual. 'But somebody did mention that she and Leo were together again.'

'Yes,' said Sarah as though she knew it too, and Robina laughed,

'That's fine by me.'

'Jimmy sends his love,' said Sarah. 'Now I'm getting to know him I think he's very nice. He's still waiting for you to come up here.'

And she would. On holidays anyway. 'Give him my love,' she said lightly, and Jimmy phoned a few times after that, and the conversations were fairly flirtatious.

Some of Robina's friends came to call. She had never invited anyone here before, but she asked Leo if she might and he seemed surprised she needed to ask. So she did, in a small way, because she had to start living her own life. She emphasised all the time that she was only here until she could move back home, and that she was helping Mrs Palmer not keeping Leo company whatever the gossips said.

She didn't do much hostessing for Leo. He was off to America in three weeks and working most nights in his study. When he brought a couple of fellow businessmen home she sat at the table with them, and they treated her as though she was the lady of the house, and it was a very pleasant meal. They were borrowing the *Achilles* and they sailed away that night, to collect their wives somewhere down the coast, and then head for the Greek islands.

Mostly she ate alone with Leo in the evenings, and she was going to miss this when the parting came because he was something special as a companion. He talked and he listened. When he listened Robina talked as she had never done to anybody. Not about her love life, but about almost everything else, without inhibition. When he talked he made her laugh, so that some nights she fell asleep still chuckling, remembering some crazy tale. And he made her think. He stretched her mind. She felt more alive when he was in the house, and the nights he didn't come home, which were probably Imogen nights, were long and dreary.

She wasn't jealous of Imogen, Leo would be another brother to her after the fifteenth, and she was looking forward immensely to living in the Castle again. But it had been really good being here with him and she wished that he was staying on for the wedding.

'No chance,' Sarah told Robina, after a phone talk with Leo the day before he was due to fly to America. 'Business comes first.' Sarah sounded resigned not bitter, and Robina said,

'Pity. Anyhow, it will be a lovely wedding.'

If the fine weather held it should be perfect, and with just over a week to go there was time for the weather to break and mend again, but yesterday and today had been oppressive, and while she was on the phone to Sarah, Robina could see dark clouds massing in the sky. Jack had said there was a storm coming up and she felt that it fitted her mood well, because she was quite depressed that Leo was going. She wasn't a hostage. He had been angry when he insisted on her staying, but she was sure now that he would let her go if she wanted to leave, and by the time he came back from his business trip she ought to have some alternative accommodation lined up.

Her headache might be due to worrying about what she should do, or simply to all this static electricity in the air. There hadn't been a bad storm here since the night the Castle burned, but even a faint rumble of thunder could make her shudder and she was apprehensive about her re-action when a real storm came.

Mrs Palmer and Jack knew what memories a storm would conjure up and she was touched by their concern. Although neither of them voiced it outright Jack gave Robina quite a worried look when he announced that they were due for a storm, and all day Mrs Palmer had been anxiously waiting for it to break. If the thunder and lightning came in daylight that would be much easier for Robina, but night fell, airless and black, and when she went to bed it seemed to her that this was exactly like that other night.

She hadn't seen much of Leo. They had eaten together, but then he had gone into the study, he was off early in the morning, he must have last-minute things to do, and she had sat with the Palmers watching a television that flashed until Jack said, 'Better turn it off,' just like Uncle Randolph had done.

When she said goodnight Mrs Palmer had asked her, 'You'll be all right?' and she'd said, 'Of course I will.' It was after midnight, she couldn't keep them up any longer, and there was no certainty that the storm was going to break.

But she lay listening for the thunder, hearing it in the distance with rising panic, until she swallowed a couple of sleeping pills from the little bottle that was still on her bedside table. She would knock herself out and then she'd know nothing till morning, and quite soon a heavy drugged sleep rolled over her like a thick blanket.

She came out of it choking and blinking in a flash of white lightning, and the terror of a nightmare was on her. Nothing was real. It was all blurred and slow motion, but she was sitting bolt upright, swaying, in the core of the storm. Lightning and thunder and smoke and fire were all around her, and through the smoke came Leo.

'It's all right,' he said, 'it's all right.'

She tried to say, 'We're on fire.'

'No.' His arms were around her and she closed her eyes and clung to him and she was warm again and safe. And almost awake. She knew she wasn't dreaming. The storm was overhead, but she was in bed with Leo and melting, floating. 'Please love me,' she said, then someone was tapping on the door, and she tried to open her eyes but her eyelids were so heavy.

There was a light in the corridor and the dark silhouette of Leo's broad shoulders in the doorway, and she heard Mrs Palmer stammering, 'Oh, I am sorry ... I thought ... I mean ... I brought her a cup of tea, I thought she might be ...'

'Thank you,' said Leo.

Robina felt no embarrassment at all. She *was* awake, but it was still like a dream. She was smiling, her limbs were soft and languorous, and she wanted his mouth, his hands, his hard strong body covering hers. She held out her arms to him, and he put down the cup and saucer on the table by the bed and came to her, and she heard him say, 'My love,' and thought he kissed her very gently. And she thought he said, 'My poor little love.'

Next morning she wasn't sure about that. She wasn't very sure about anything next morning. Last night was hazy, but she could recall enough of it to bring the hot blood to her cheeks. She knew that Leo had been here, she was very sure of that, but she had no idea when he left. She was alone in her large bed now, and it was time she was up, and through the window the sky was a washed-out grey so the storm was over.

An empty cup and saucer was on the bedside table. Mrs Palmer *had* brought a cup of tea and handed it in to Leo, and Robina must have drunk it, and she had better start explaining. She caught Mrs Palmer in the kitchen, alone which was lucky, and said very quickly, 'I want to apologise about last night. I took a couple of sleeping pills, but the storm still gave me a nightmare. I seem to have disturbed half the house.'

Mrs Palmer smiled, and Robina blushed even hotter because Mrs Palmer had her own ideas why Leo had answered her knock on Robina's door last night, and talking about nightmares wasn't going to change them.

'He's on his way to the airport now,' said Mrs Palmer.

'The house is never the same without him.' And Robina couldn't pretend, even to herself, that she wasn't going to miss Leo. As Mrs Palmer spoke she felt a sharp sense of loss because he hadn't said goodbye and a sick and empty feeling because he had gone.

Half the guests were needing overnight accommodation. Some were staying here, some with friends, a few in hotels around. Robina was organising most of that. She hardly had a quiet moment, and yet she did some quiet thinking.

She was missing Leo all the time, so that every day showed her over and over again how important he had become to her. There was Imogen, of course, and Imogen was a dazzling rival, but perhaps he wasn't all that hooked on cool elegant women, because he had admired the red dress and he seemed to enjoy Robina's company. He laughed with her, he liked her. She wasn't deeply in love herself but the thought of him loving her made her toes curl, and when he came back she would still be here, and maybe they could carry on from that last night, wherever that had ended ...

Sarah and Chris arrived the day before the wedding. Chris's TV team, with one wife and one girl-friend, were in two cars behind, and as they all scrambled out Robina greeted them with squeals of joy. Jimmy enveloped her in a great hug and she saw Mrs Palmer's eyebrows go up, and after that she went round kissing them all to show there was nothing special about Jimmy.

It was last-minute touches today, the flower arrangements, the preparing of the buffet tables. All was bustle and laughter, and Sarah was going to make the prettiest bride.

She had brought her wedding outfit with her, a cream silk suit because 'I have to have something I'm going to get some wear out of, don't I? I mean, it's no good me choosing something wild I'm never going to wear again.'

She showed it to Robina, in her bedroom, and as she stroked the material she said with downcast eyes, 'I think of Tony a lot,' her first husband, 'and how different Chris is, and how lucky I am. He's so good to me, and I'll be good for him, I promise you.'

'I'm sure you will,' said Robina, and somehow now it didn't seem all that unlikely. 'Put the suit on,' she coaxed. 'Do let me see you in it.'

Sarah looked ravishingly pretty—she would have looked pretty in a sack—and Robina was making admiring noises when the transistor that had been playing music switched on to the news bulletin. Among the headlines was a plane crash in America, and between the first statement, and the fuller details which proved that Leo could not have been involved, everything was blotted out for Robina. Sarah was still admiring herself in the mirror, she hadn't even heard the news, but for Robina it had been a moment of blind black terror. She had been scared half to death, and that was another sign how much Leo mattered to her.

He phoned that evening. He hadn't phoned the house before, but he wanted to talk to Sarah and Chris and wish them well for tomorrow, and then he spoke to Robina. She didn't know whether he asked for her, but Sarah handed over the receiver and Robina said gaily, 'Hello. We're fine here, no problems.'

'I'm sure you are,' he said, 'but don't run yourself into the ground.'

He didn't say anything in particular. It was the sort of conversation anybody could have listened to, and never guessed that Leo Morgan's last sight of Robina had been when he got out of her bed and left her sleeping. But his voice did strange things to her, and even while she was chattering in reply her mouth felt dry and she kept thinking how nice it would have been if he had used an endearment. Called her 'my love' perhaps, as she thought he had when the storm was raging.

He didn't. He said, 'Goodbye, Bina,' and nobody else used that pet name, but he didn't know that, he didn't mean anything by it. Robina wondered if he phoned Imogen regularly and how he talked to her, and wished that something would stop Imogen turning up tomorrow.

'All right?' asked Chris as she put down the receiver, and she turned a blank face to him. 'Of course. Why?'

'You look worried,' he said.

'Well, I'm not,' and she smiled to prove it, because she could hardly explain that every time Imogen Faulkner came into her mind she found herself sighing.

The ceremony was nearly over next day when Robina blinked away a hint of tears and turned her head and saw Imogen just across the aisle. Imogen smiled, and for some reason Robina felt as shaken as though she had burst out laughing. It was the kind of smile you looked away from, feeling apprehensive, and she had more than a hunch that Imogen would spoil the day for her if she could, so she kept out of Miss Faulkner's way when the guests went back to the Morgan home.

There were enough people milling around to provide a barrier, and Robina dodged whenever she saw Imogen coming towards her. It was a very successful reception. The weather was perfect and the buffet was excellent and everyone seemed to be enjoying themselves.

Sarah gave Mrs Palmer and Robina a final hug each before she and Chris drove away. 'I shall ring Leo tonight and tell him what a super party he missed.' She climbed into the car and called through the wound-down window to Robina, 'Or will you be ringing him?'

'Yes, I can,' Robina promised, and Sarah settled back, nestling against Chris's shoulder.

'I won't bother, then. See some of you in a week's time,'
and off the newlyweds went.

As the little crowd moved away from the drive, to the
house or the gardens, Robina felt a hand through her arm
and Imogen said, 'I've hardly had chance of a word with
you.'

She was holding tight, there was to be no shaking her off,
so the only thing to do was carry on walking and keep smiling. Imogen was smiling, and talking in a sweet false voice.
'You have worked hard, haven't you? I'm sure Leo will be
delighted with you.' She repeated, 'Delighted,' with a small
grimace. 'I wonder if they'll put that under his picture
again.' She was talking about the gossip column. 'We certainly got a laugh out of that.'

'Did we?' said Robina tautly. 'And who's we?'

'Leo and I, of course.'

'Of course.' Inside she felt like a block of ice.

'You're a very funny girl,' said Imogen, as though this
was a compliment and Robina was a professional comic.
'Sometimes Leo keeps me giggling half the night with
tales about you.'

He talked about her to Imogen? Robina remembered the
things she had told him and there was nothing that funny,
surely, but to a cynical listener she might have sounded
foolish sometimes. And the time he'd asked if he could
come to her room. He would hardly have told Imogen that,
but he could have said that a casual compliment or a hand
on her arm had sparked off the hysterics. It would be easy
to make that amusing, Robina hopping around screaming,
'Don't touch me!'

It was like fireworks going off in her head. Flash after
flash. Even the night before he went, the time she had
begged, 'Please love me.' He hadn't phoned here till he
wanted to speak to Sarah, but he had probably phoned

Imogen. Imogen had the smug look of someone who knew everything, and she wasn't holding Robina's arm any more because Robina was standing still, in the deserted drive, with no one else near enough to hear.

'You don't need to phone and tell him all about today,' said Imogen. 'I can deliver any messages. I'll be seeing him tomorrow, I'm flying out to join him. I only stopped for the wedding, and I'm so glad I did because you've managed everything beautifully. By the way, what are you going to do with yourself now?' She had stopped smiling. 'I know that Leo's sorry for you, that's why he's letting you keep some of the Castle, and I know you're an in-law now, but I shall be coming back here with him and I would rather you weren't still around.'

Robina almost said she was here because she had been ordered to stay, but instead she heard herself snap, 'Oh, push off,' and Imogen glared.

'We'll phone from America and give you notice to quit!'

'You do that,' said Robina. She went into the first marquee and drained a glass of champagne, then she looked around for Jimmy and told him, 'I think I might go back with you.'

He was driving back to London tonight and there was a spare seat in his car. 'That's a splendid idea,' he said. 'You come and have a holiday.'

'Just a holiday, is it?' asked Mrs Palmer, following Robina upstairs when she went to pack, and Robina stopped pretending and admitted,

'I'll probably get a job up there, and I'm sure Leo isn't going to raise any objections, because you were wrong about the other night, you know. He came to see if I was all right because of the storm, like you did, and I'd taken two sleeping pills and I'm not used to the things so they knocked me stupid. But all he did was make sure I was all right and then he went. It's Miss Faulkner, not me.'

'Smug cow,' said Mrs Palmer, surprisingly, and Robina grinned.

'She is, isn't she? I'll have to borrow a case.'

Mrs Palmer brought her a case of Sarah's, and then went away shaking her head, and Robina made a quick job of the packing. She daren't linger up here on her own or she would collapse in a heap of misery, or even change her mind and hang on until she got that phone call from America. Or until Leo came home with Imogen.

She didn't want to leave. She knew now that she had stayed because she wanted to, not because she had believed that Leo would harm Chris. She was in fathoms deeper than she had ever imagined, so that leaving this house would be like being torn from the arms of her lover.

She loved him, passionately and completely, and she didn't believe he had made her sound such a fool as Imogen tried to make out. But he had talked about her to Imogen, and they had smiled together at that newspaper story, and Imogen was joining him tomorrow.

Robina didn't think he would ask her to leave this house, she could probably stay until her apartment was ready, but the most she could expect from him in the way of loving was a visit to her room, because Leo Morgan was not a one-woman man, and she couldn't settle for that.

If she kept a few hundred miles between them there would be less risk of her coming when he called. She had always answered when he called 'Bina,' and as she closed the case and pressed down the lid another memory surfaced, of Leo calling, 'Bina, are you all right?' She had responded through two sleeping pills to his voice. He had woken her, not the storm, and if she stayed in this house she had no more chance of resisting him than a needle of holding back from a magnet, and she snapped the fasteners of the case and carried it down into the hall.

Even when Chris and Sarah came back from their honeymoon there would probably be a spare room for her. Friends of Chris were always dossing down in the rabbit-warren of an upper floor that was his home. Laura, his ex-girl-friend, had a permanent bed-sitter there, although she and Chris had split up months ago.

Laura let Robina in, by the cool light of dawn, when Jimmy's car drew up outside the house. Robina had been asleep in the back, and she climbed out of the car yawning; she had been awake until the last half hour of the journey when sheer exhaustion had closed her eyes. The moment she opened them she remembered she was leaving Leo, so that when she stopped yawning she had to bite her lip to stop herself whimpering.

Laura looked sleepy too; it was very early in the morning. She was wearing a man's brown dressing gown, tied round the waist, and she smiled blearily at Robina who had phoned her earlier.

'I'll pick you up for lunch,' said Jimmy, and Robina nodded. 'Can you manage that?' He put the case on the pavement and Robina said,

'Yes, of course. Thanks for the lift.'

'Nice girl, isn't she?' said Laura, leading the way up the dark staircase.

'Sarah? Yes, she is.'

'I'm working most of tomorrow,' said Laura. 'I've got this TV part I told you about, but I'm glad you've come up, we'll be able to get around together.' She dug a key out of her pocket as she reached her own doorway, and handed it over to Robina.

It opened Chris and Sarah's apartment, and Robina went straight to bed and cried herself to sleep. It was a relief to be able to cry and it didn't matter if the pillow got soaked because she had a week to dry it out. But when she woke with swollen eyes she wished that she had held back some of the tears. They hadn't helped much. It still seemed a black sunken world, desolate as a lost planet, and she still felt as though all the fight had been knocked out of her.

She had thought she could fight Imogen and that perhaps, just perhaps, she might win. But there would always be another Imogen, another Robina. Leo Morgan did not make permanent commitments, he was not a marrying man. He would have made love to Robina that night he'd asked if he might come to her room, but today he would be meeting Imogen, and tonight he would be loving her, and thinking about that hurt so badly that hell couldn't be much worse.

Jealousy was tearing her to pieces, and there was no way she could contemplate a lifetime of it.

Laura banged on the door of the living room, found it unlocked and walked in. 'I've brought you a cup of tea. I'm off to the studios now.' She came through the open bedroom door and gave a squeal of horror when she saw Robina's puffy face and pink eyes. 'Oh, you look *terrible*!'

Robina sniffed and reached for her handbag, beside the bed, and hunted for a tissue. 'I seem to have managed to catch a cold somehow.' She buried her nose in the tissue. 'Thanks for the tea. It looks a lovely day.'

You could see the sunshine, but it wasn't going to be a lovely day, and Laura said she was late, she had to dash, and there were some aspirins in the bathroom cabinet and perhaps Robina should take a couple because she looked as though she was running a temperature.

As soon as she had gone Robina scrambled out of bed and tried to repair the damage. She bathed her face and put cold compresses on her eyes, then made up, and by the time Jimmy arrived to take her out to lunch she looked almost normal. Another thing she was resolved on, there were going to be no more tears.

She wished she hadn't agreed to spend what was left of

this day with Jimmy, although she liked him well enough, because it wasn't fair to let him think she might have come up here to be with him.

It was a Saturday, he wasn't working, and they had lunch in a pub by the river. Then they walked through Kew Gardens, and in the evening went to the theatre on the green, and afterwards to supper in a little restaurant he knew.

He did most of the talking and Robina smiled and nodded, and enjoyed being with him, but would have been as happy with any other friend. As happy with another girl. There was only a pale spark of the zest life had with Leo, and not a hint of the physical undercurrents that threatened her so overwhelmingly when Leo was near.

Over coffee, after supper, she said she was going back to Chris's flat; and although Jimmy was obviously set on going up with her all he would be getting was more coffee, or a drink if Chris and Sarah had left any around. And a quiet thank-you kiss and goodnight.

Lights were on all over the house, televisions were still playing and you could hear voices. Laura's door was wide open and as Robina reached it Laura jumped up from a chair placed so that she could see anyone passing by. 'Hey!' she called. 'There's someone waiting for you.'

'Who?' Robina asked.

'I don't know,' said Laura. 'But if you don't want him come back and tell me.'

It could be anybody. There was only one man it couldn't be, but she ran along the passage and Leo was standing by Chris's empty fireplace, glaring from under heavy black brows. He looked like he had when the car broke down and she hadn't phoned to tell him Sarah was safe. She was trying to escape from him, he was the last man in the world she wanted here. But her heart soared and sang when she saw him.

'You're in America,' she said stupidly.

'Am I?' Obviously plans had been changed and he'd flown back early, but what had brought him here in this thunderous mood?

Jimmy was right behind her. He followed as she went into the room and she said, 'Leo Morgan, James Allman.'

'Goodnight, Mr Allman,' said Leo grimly. He came towards Jimmy, Robina didn't think he touched him, but Jimmy backed out of the room and the door was closed; and she knew that outside Jimmy was wondering what had happened and whether he should open the door again. But she knew he wouldn't.

The room could have been tidier, and through an open door was the unmade bed. She hadn't bothered before she went out this morning, and she wished now that she had, if only to show Leo that Sarah's new home wasn't too awful.

It must be something awful that had brought him here, something that was making him look haggard, and she thought, There's been an accident. Chris and Sarah in that car—Chris can be a mad driver. She croaked, 'What is it? Has something terrible happened?'

'No,' he said, 'and it isn't going to. I've come to fetch you.'

'Fetch me?' she echoed, and then shrilled, 'Take me back, you mean? Oh, forget it. You're not going to harm Chris and Sarah, you don't need a hostage, and anyway, I think they'll make out.'

'That's up to them, and right now I couldn't care less.' So he must have come for her because he wanted her, and Leo Morgan always got what he wanted, and if Robina had cared less she would have been happy enough to go with him.

She gripped the nearest thing, the edge of the table, and hung on and said, 'I came here to get away from you.'

'Do you still blame me for your uncle's death?'

'No ...' Of course she didn't, she couldn't believe that she ever had.

'Then why won't you let me love you?'

'Because——' She moistened her dry lips. She couldn't say, 'Because it would be sex for you and love for me and I am the one whose heart would get smashed.' She said instead, and harshly, 'Because I don't think in the long run it would be a good idea. Because I do not want it.'

She held the table tighter to stop her hands reaching for him. It seemed that every nerve in her was calling out, while Leo stood watching, dark eyes hooded, and she thought, He knows he could take me so easily, he knows I asked him to make love to me. She began to babble, 'The night before you went, the storm, I remember what I said, but I'd taken sleeping pills and——'

'I saw the bottle,' he said. 'And I'm surprised you remember who I was. You were just talking in your sleep.'

She was, but she had wanted him sleeping or waking. 'How—long did you stay?'

'Until the storm passed. But don't worry, not in your bed. You slept like a log, and I sat in a chair and drank your cup of tea.'

'That was very kind of you.' She edged round the table and wondered if she could close the bedroom door, but decided it was best to ignore it. 'Could I get you a cup of tea now?' Her voice was twittering, her hands fluttering, 'Or a drink? There's surely something.' She knelt down on the fur rug in front of the sideboard cupboard, and opened the door on a tin of lager and half a bottle of peppermint cordial.

'No, thank you,' said Leo.

'Just as well.' She was desperately trying to keep the talk trivial. 'The wedding went off beautifully. Sarah looked beautiful. It was such a shame you missed it.'

'Was it?'

'I suppose she's my sister now, isn't she? I shall like that. I suppose you're my brother.'

'There is no way,' said Leo, 'that you and I are ever going to be brother and sister.'

'Why not?' Robina jumped up, brushing her skirt which had white hairs on it from the goatskin rug. It sounded like something from an old-fashioned romance, I'll always be a sister to you. 'Why can't we be?' she asked, and before she could move or speak again she was in his arms and his mouth was on hers, and hunger for him came so overwhelmingly that she responded with a savage passion, but almost at once tried to turn her head away.

The kiss went on and the warm sweet closeness flooded her, drowning her, but she held herself rigid and when he stopped she looked up at him with agonised eyes. 'That's why not,' he said. He knew he could stir the depths of her sensuality until she was beyond reason but that she was still fighting him and herself. 'And one day,' he said, 'I'm going to get inside your head and break down whatever it is in there that's screaming at me to keep away.'

'*Why?* It can't matter that much that one woman says no.' Perhaps she was the first, perhaps that was why he had to break her. Imogen certainly hadn't said no. 'What about Imogen?' she demanded.

'What about her?'

'Well, you're here. She was flying out to join you today.'

'First I've heard of it,' he said.

'You mean you didn't know?'

'I did not. We probably passed in mid-air.'

That made her smile, that and the thought that if Imogen had lied about this she could have lied about other things. She said, 'She was at the wedding. She told me you'd had many a laugh together over me.'

'You believed her?' Leo sounded aghast and she said quietly,

'It seemed possible. You still see her a lot.'

'And who told you that?'

'She did. And other people did.'

Other people who had listened to Imogen. 'We've met,' said Leo. 'Not by appointment and certainly not by design on my part. But we've never been alone together since she left my house that night, and I would never in any circumstances discuss you with her. Or with anyone else.'

'Oh,' she said, 'I'm glad about that.'

She was more than glad. She was delirious with joy. The next time he kissed her there would be no holding back. She sat down on the sofa because it would be a good place to be if her legs gave way, and waited for him to come and sit beside her.

But he stayed on his feet, and asked, 'Did it matter to you, Imogen saying she was flying out to join me?'

'Yes,' she said promptly.

'Good. Then you might have some idea how I felt when Mrs P. told me last night that you'd gone with the man who kept ringing you, and you weren't coming back. You'd said you were staying at your brother's, she said, but she knew he'd got his eye on you.'

'Were you back last night?' she asked.

'She phoned me. I flew back today, I'm returning tomorrow.'

It sounded as though what Mrs Palmer had told him had brought him back, which was a staggering thought, and she gasped, 'You didn't come just to talk to me?'

'Yes.'

'But you could have talked to me on the phone.'

'You could have put a phone down,' he said succinctly. 'I'm not so easily put down.'

'I can't take it in.' Robina laughed a little, incredulously. 'Sarah said you'd never walk to the end of the street after anyone.'

'I'd follow you to the end of any street.' He came then and stood looking down at her, very tall, very dark, and she felt his power and knew how far-reaching it was. 'I'd have found you,' he said softly, 'if I'd ended up crawling to reach you.'

She stood no chance in the world of getting away, his pursuit of her would have been implacable, and she wouldn't have run if she could and perhaps she didn't care what happened to her afterwards. But all this just to collect another woman! She said with a touch of bitterness, 'It isn't going to be that big a deal, possessing me,' and she smiled wryly, but he didn't smile. He said,

'It's going to be the biggest deal of all. Sometimes when you look at me you still see the pirate, but when I look at you I see my wife.'

'Your *wife*?' she gasped.

'One day you'll think about marrying me.'

She had known he wanted her as a lover, but she had never realised he meant for ever, and she heard herself stammer, 'How long have you——?' before the words trailed away.

'How long have I known I was in love with you?' Leo said 'love' as though it was something accepted and understood, by him at any rate. She nodded, and he sat down beside her then, brow furrowed like a man trying to give a straight and serious answer. 'Maybe in the Castle that morning,' he said at last. 'When I realised what a close thing it had been, you getting out from that fire, I thought, I might never have known her. And having you there, warm and breathing, seemed something to be so thankful for that I could have gone down on my knees.'

He had held out his arms to her, in the burned-out kitchens, when she had been shaking, and she had felt his strength flowing into her. For her too that had been the beginning of love.

'But when I knew for sure,' he said, 'was when the fog held you up that night. I phoned everywhere, every place I thought you might be, and then every police station, every hospital. You'd got to have had an accident. When you finally drove up——'

'You looked as though you wanted to shake me.'

'I did. Shake you and kiss you.'

'I thought you were only worried about Sarah.' He had turned on Robina demanding, 'Where the hell have you been?' But that was what you did to the ones you loved, only you usually went on to shriek, 'I've been worried out of my mind about you!'

'I was concerned about Sarah, of course,' he said, 'but it was you.' His dark eyes were filled with such a blaze of love that she could hardly meet them. 'And God knows it will always be you. When you told me Sarah was marrying your brother the thing that hit me first was that you'd known what was going on and you hadn't told me.'

'I didn't,' she said, quickly and breathlessly. 'Honestly. I just didn't.' He began to smile.

'The next thing was that you'd be leaving if Sarah married and I couldn't let you go,' and she smiled too.

'You needed a hostage?'

'I needed time. You'd got this backlog of prejudice against me that I was hoping to wear down, little by little. I didn't even phone you while I was away. I hoped you might phone me, and when you didn't I waited until I could speak to Sarah so that it all seemed casual. Then Mrs P. told me you'd cleared off and I knew the waiting game wasn't working.'

He had been *scared* to speak to her! That was nearly as crazy as the way she had carried on. She said, 'When you asked if you could come to my room, you remember?'

'Very well,' he said wryly.

'Well, it wasn't that I was still seeing you as the pirate. It was because I'd just been told you were still seeing Imogen, but as I was living in your house I was handier.'

'Who told you that?'

Whoever it was could have made a dangerous enemy, his face was granite-hard, and Robina shrugged. She was naming no names because it didn't matter. She said, 'Well, you've come to my room now,' and went into his arms, and he kissed her slowly and fully, with deep true passion, and as she lay quietly beside him he murmured,

'Say you love me.'

'I love you,' she whispered.

'And you'll fly out with me tomorrow? I'm there for another three weeks. We could get married out there, or as soon as we get back.' When she shook her head Leo said, 'Please,' huskily. 'Please, Bina, I beg you, come with me.'

She didn't want him humble and pleading. 'All that's stopping me,' she explained, 'is that I don't have a passport, and even you can't fix that by tomorrow, can you?'

'No.' His breath was warm on her cheek, his hand was light on her breast, and his nearness was driving her distracted. 'But I'll tell you what I can do by tomorrow. I can prove to you that I'm worth waiting for, so you'll be at the airport when I fly in.'

She looked up at him with a flash of mischief in her eyes. 'Now how do you propose to do that?'

'I'll show you,' he said, and he got up and locked the door. Then he came back to the sofa and swung her up in his arms and carried her, warm and yielding, into the other room.

Mills & Boon Classics

The very best of Mills & Boon
romances, brought back for those of you
who missed reading them when they
were first published.

In
October
we bring back the following four
great romantic titles.

NO QUARTER ASKED
by Janet Dailey

Stacy Adams was a rich girl who wanted to sample real life for
a change, so she courageously took herself off alone to Texas
for a while. It was obvious from the first that the arrogant
rancher Cord Harris, for some reason, disapproved of her — but
why should she care what he thought?

MIRANDA'S MARRIAGE
by Margery Hilton

Desperation forced Miranda to encamp for the night in Jason
Steele's office suite, but unfortunately he found her there, and
after the unholy wrath that resulted she never dreamed that a
few months later she would become his wife. For Jason was
reputed to be a rake where women were concerned. So what
chance of happiness had Miranda?

THE LIBRARY TREE
by Lilian Peake

Carolyn Lyle was the niece of a very influential man, and
nothing would convince her new boss, that iceberg Richard
Hindon, that she was nothing but a spoiled, pampered darling
who couldn't be got rid of fast enough! Had she even got time
to make him change his mind about her?

PALACE OF THE POMEGRANATE
by Violet Winspear

Life had not been an easy ride for Grace Wilde and she had
every reason to be distrustful of men. Then, in the Persian
desert, she fell into the hands of another man. Kharim Khan,
who was different from any other man she had met . . .

Doctor Nurse Romances

and October's
stories of romantic relationships behind the scenes
of modern medical life are:

SURGEON'S CHALLENGE
by Helen Upshall

Sister Claire Tyndall's success as a nurse was undoubted
— but as a woman? Richard Lynch and Dr Alan Jarvis
both made it clear that they were interested in her. Both
were handsome and determined, but both — unfortunately
for Claire — seemed to be married already!

ATTACHED TO DOCTOR MARCHMONT
by Juliet Shore

Doctor Sally Preston's relationship with her new chief,
Darien Marchmont, got off to a sticky start. So she was
less than pleased to discover that their first joint
assignment was a two-man medical survey in the heart
of the North African desert!

The Mills & Boon Rose is the Rose of Romance

Look for the Mills & Boon Rose next month

IMAGES OF LOVE *by Anne Mather*
Tobie couldn't resist seeing Robert Lang again, to exact her
revenge — but she didn't know what had happened to Robert
since they had last met . . .

BRAND OF POSSESSION *by Carole Mortimer*
Jake Weston's lack of trust in her ought to have killed all the
love Stacy felt for him — but it didn't.

DIFFICULT DECISION *by Janet Dailey*
Deborah knew that her job as secretary to the forceful Zane
Wilding would be difficult — but the real challenge was to her
emotions . . .

HANNAH *by Betty Neels*
Nurse Hannah Lang was happy to accompany the van Eysink's
back to Holland, but the unbending Doctor Valentijn van Bertes
was not quite so enthusiastic about it.

A SECRET AFFAIR *by Lilian Peake*
As a confidential secretary, Alicia was well aware how essential
it was to keep secret about her boss's new project. So why didn't
he trust her?

THE WILD MAN *by Margaret Rome*
Rebel soon realised how Luiz Manchete had earned his name —
the wild man — when she found herself alone with him in the
heart of his jungle kingdom . . .

STRANGER IN THE NIGHT *by Charlotte Lamb*
When Clare met Macey Janson, she began to lose some of her
fear of men. So why did Luke Murry have to turn up again,
making Macey suspect the worst of her?

RACE AGAINST LOVE *by Sally Wentworth*
Toni disliked Adam Yorke intensely, and her friend Carinna was
more than welcome to him! But did Toni *really* mean that?

DECEPTION *by Margaret Pargeter*
Sick to death of being run after for her money, Thea ran away
herself — but she only found a new set of problems . . .

FROZEN HEART *by Daphne Clair*
Joining an expedition to the Antarctic, Kerin was taken aback to
discover that the arrogant Dain Ransome was to be its leader . . .

If you have difficulty in obtaining any of these books from your
local paperback retailer, write to:

Mills & Boon Reader Service
P.O. Box 236, Thornton Road, Croydon, Surrey, CR9 3RU.

Available November 1980